All the Right Places

Short Stories by
Wayne Goodman

"Population Maintenace" appeared in *Off the Rocks, Volume 18* (NewTown Writers Press, 2014)

"Nice Day for a Picnic" appeared (in part) in *The Wells Street Journal, Issue Nine* (University of Westminster, 2018)

"Noah's Raft" appeared in *Off the Rocks, Volume 19* (NewTown Writers Press, 2015)

"Out of Yoshiwara" appeared in *Best Gay Erotica of the Year, Volume 4* (Cleis Press, 2018)

Version 1.0

11 February 2020

ISBN: 978-1-7344700-0-0

Library of Congress Control Number: 2020930081

waynegoodmanbooks

waynegoodmanbooks@gmail.com
Twitter: @WGoodmanbooks

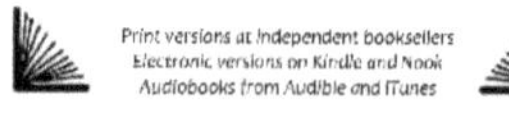

Dedication

To begin with, I must thank my partner, Rick May, who is the first to hear anything I've written. His support and guidance have helped me to be the writer I have become.

Next, my appreciation goes to those editors who read my drafts and decided to include my stories in their publications. Also, those editors who read my drafts and decided not to include my works.

My deepest appreciation to the Benicia Outlaw Writers Group, my partners in literary crime.

Table of Contents

Population Maintenance 1

Manscapes........................... 11

Welcome to ViReLand 29

Closest to the Jack 45

Rumpspringa........................... 55

Looking for Love in All the Right Places ... 83

Stag Station 107

"Nice Day for a Picnic" 131

Noah's Raft 155

Sunday/Sinday........................ 177

Out of Yoshiwara 193

Population Maintenance

Off the Rocks put out a call for submissions, asking for stories that dealt with the word "gay." Something stuck in my mind about using the word in an advertising slogan and linking it to the topic of overpopulation. Of course, many of us who identify as "gay" have reproduced (and I am one of them), but this is speculative fiction, and anything/everything is possible.

Population Maintenance,
Redefining 'Gay' at Oldner, Barnes, Gary, Young & Niedermeyer

"It's Sapient To Be Homo!"

The poster showed a happy couple, two women, smiling at each other.

"Reduce or Maintain the Surface Population," commanded the line at the bottom.

"That's plagiarism!" shouted Sheila Barnes in her last-season, off-black, faux wool power suit. "We can't use that. Besides, we're supposed to be promoting population maintenance, not homosexuality."

"But Sheila," Marjorie whined, "that book is almost a hundred years old and the author is long dead. Who's going to know?"

"*I* know," she pointed to herself, "and that's all that matters. I don't want Anthony Burgess's heirs or his estate coming after us."

"What if we change the slogan to 'Be a Homo Sapien!'?" Marjorie looked at Sheila for a response.

The boss's eyes raised to the tops of their sockets. "Not any better. And it really doesn't address the issue. Besides, Marie and I adopted a kid last week. Just because you're a same-sex couple doesn't mean you can't have children." She looked along the sides of the meeting table at the other pairs of ad writers. "Who's next?"

Tom raised his hand and Sheila nodded. Tom and his partner, Paul, moved to the end of the table and placed their proposed campaign poster on the stand.

"Reproduction," Paul pointed and Tom read along, "Is For the Birds." Beneath was a drawing of a nest crowded with cartoon robins, one baby falling out and the mama robin not even noticing it. "And Bees." With a cartoon swarm of bees hovering around an overpopulated hive. They both looked at Sheila.

"Hate it! Hate it!" she screamed "Hate it!"

Tom and Paul cowered, grabbed the poster and ran back to their seats.

"Who's next?" Sheila shouted.

Emma, sweet-faced and naïve-looking, held up a placard. "Go forth, be fruitless. Don't multiply!" it admonished. The picture was Eve tempting Adam with an apple in the Garden of Eden, next to the Tree of Knowledge.

"Too Biblical." Sheila shook her head. "Too literal. Too… wrong."

Emma put away her attempt at pleasing the boss and looked down at her hands.

Sheila banged on the table with her fist. "The Population Maintenance Information Network is going to be deciding in a week who will be the lead ad agency on this campaign. Is this the best you lamebrains can come up with? We work for Oldner, Barnes, Gary, Young & Niedermeyer, people. You play for the major leagues now. If you can't come up with a winning marketing strategy, I'm firing the whole lot of you!" Her red face began to moisten with perspiration.

"Sheila," Frank raised his hand, "I believe we might have just what you want. It's patriotic and makes good use of a national hero." His partner Phil smiled in support.

"Oh, really," she looked at him with mock anticipation. "You have my full attention. Pitch away."

Frank stood. "You know that George Washington–frequently referred to as the Father of our County–never had any children of his own."

"I like it, Frank, I think I like it," Sheila boomed out.

"So instead of having him chop down the cherry tree as a kid–"

"I'm going to stop you right there, Frank. Sit down."

"But you haven't even seen our concept."

"I don't need to Frank. Sit down. Shut up."

"Honestly, Sheila," Marjorie stood up. "We've all worked very hard in a very short time to come up with ideas for this campaign. Perhaps you could grace us with your eminent brilliance and share one of your delectable crumbs with us." Heads around the table nodded in agreement.

"You know," Sheila started, "you guys get paid to come up with the ideas." She pointed at the others, then to herself. "I get paid to edit them. It is not my job to do your job."

"We're not really following what you want from us here," Frank chimed in. "Can't you even suggest some idea of what you're looking for?"

Sheila closed her eyes slowly, breathed in slowly, exhaled slowly. Then she looked at the lot again, "It's very simple. Same as always. A catchy slogan, an eye-grabbing graphic, and an informative tagline. One, two, three. Our time-tested method that has worked from days immemorial to today, tomorrow, a thousand years from now. Is it really that difficult to be clever about sexuality and reproduction?" She glanced at each person individually.

"So you want," Frank asked sarcastically, "something like 'Have Sex, Not Babies' with a picture of a pan-sexual orgy?"

"That's a good start," she pointed at him.

"Oh, for the love of…" he trailed off.

"No, really," Sheila continued. "That's the basic idea: people should continue to enjoy being sexual with each other, just stop having so many babies. It's that simple." She surveyed the room. "Any other pitches?"

Heads drooped, eyes averted.

One hand raised. "Yes, Myrtle," Sheila announced. "Let's see what you have to offer."

The thirty-something Myrtle in a sensible, button-down stood up holding a placard proclaiming, "Sex Good, Babies Bad." The simple, large, bold font would have grabbed the reader's attention.

"Hell, no!" Sheila screamed. Myrtle curdled and sat down. "It sounds like something out of *1984*, and I mean the book, not the year." Some people laughed at the little joke.

"Can we just open the table to discussion," Tom suggested, "Perhaps some old-school brain-storming might help. The old run-it-up-the-flagpole method." A few people nodded along.

"I'll give you five minutes, then I have another meeting." Sheila perused the blank faces staring back at her.

Paul nudged Tom, who then spoke up, "Well, as members of the Gay Community–"

"Now there's a phrase I haven't heard in a long time," Sheila interrupted. "No one talks about being 'Gay' anymore, people. We are all 'people' now, just 'people.' Not 'gay' people or 'straight' people, 'bisexual,' 'inter/trans/non' whatever."

"But look at this," Tom said as Paul touched his display on the tabletop. A thesaurus page popped up for everyone to see. "Gay used to mean glad, jolly, keen, sparkling, wild–carefree. Kind of like when you don't have children at home to raise." He looked around and smiled. Some of the others giggled along.

Paul pressed another button. "And here," Tom continued, "the word has been used as a descriptive adjective for hundreds of years." He pointed to some of the phrases hovering over the table. "A '*gay* man' was once a guy who couldn't keep it in his pants with women, a '*gay* woman' used to mean a sex worker, and the '*gay* house' was where she plied her trade. Remember 'The Gay Divorcee,' 'The Gay Blade,' 'The Gay Deceivers'? Nietzsche wrote a book called *The Gay Science* that dealt with the proper skills needed to write poetry." He paused to look around the room. Everyone else seemed to be absorbed in thought, pondering what they had just heard. "In fact, it was only about 100 years ago that people began calling homosexuals 'gay.'"

Marjorie asked, "Didn't school kids around 50 years ago start using, 'That's so gay,' to mean something was stupid, boring or generally undesirable." Heads nodded.

"Exactly!" Tom pointed at her. They took it upon themselves to put a new and different definition–albeit it somewhat negative–on a familiar expression.

"Okay, Tom, what's your point?" Sheila interjected.

"The point is, Sheila," he stared right at her, "We can reclaim the word 'Gay' for a new cause for a new era. Yes, it can still mean all those things it used to, but let's add another arrow to its quiver. Let's redefine it to mean obeying the suggested rules from the Population Maintenance Information Network. We can recycle this old chestnut and slap on a new coat of paint, brand it for the contemporary scene using the same, old word. We can make it refer to, for instance–and I'm just spit-ballin' here–a childless couple or one who adopts."

Sheila nodded with understanding. "Like, 'It's Okay to be Gay.'"

"Not my style," Tom evaluated, "but I think we can work with that."

"Good!" Sheila acknowledged. "Now, get me 15 sets of ads using the redefined 'gay' by the time I get back from my other meeting." She stood and walked through the set of double doors behind her.

Cries of "Thank you, Tom," arose from the others around the table.

"Well, let's get to work, then, people." Tom suggested. "Any ideas?"

Manscapes

I wish I could recall the origin of this story, but I cannot. It might have been a call for submission, but I don't remember.

This tale deals with the endless search for the perfect mate, even in the proximate future.

Manscapes:
Your Perfect Lover

I could hardly sleep because of all the anticipation. This morning my new… my new… (what?)… partner?… would be delivered.

Last month I saw the ad for "Manscapes," a new, fully-functional, artificial lover. At first, I worried that it might be like that old movie with the automaton wives, but the technician assured me these guys could adapt and learn, becoming the perfect partner. Okay, nobody's perfect, but at least he'd be better than the string of losers I'd endured over the last few years.

Even my morning tea could not calm me down. I checked myself in the hallway full-length mirror. Still viable after all these years. Could use a bit more tone and definition, but at least I've still got all my own hair, and its original color (with a little help from dye). Perhaps I should have considered spending the money on rejuvenative surgery, but I reasoned what was the good of looking better if the guys you met were still rejects.

I paced back and forth by the bay window, looking down over Castro Street for the delivery van. People walked along the sidewalk, cars zoomed to and fro. A bus. A scooter.

At precisely nine o'clock, the buzzer sounded its annoying loud hum from below. I had left my home as original as possible, and I chose not to install a modern security system with a view screen. I pressed the century-old, wobbly talk button and asked who it was.

"Delivery," came the curt, but masculine, reply.

I pressed the door release, and the sound of the remote hum and mechanical clack of the lock made my dick swell a little. From the top of the stairs I could see a dark shadow lifting a large, rectangular box, about the size of a refrigerator, up to me. At least if any of the nosy neighbors wondered what I had gotten, it looked something like a new appliance.

Once he reached the top, I got a look at the delivery guy's face. He was kind of cute. About my age, with a headful of curly dark blond hair.

"Marks?" he asked.

"It's Marques, pronounced like Marcus." I had this trouble all the time.

"Oh, sorry. I have your delivery here." He indicated the large cardboard container. "Where is your high voltage?"

I was kind of old-fashioned about certain things and did not like electric clothes dryers. The building had been piped for natural gas, and I used that instead. The high-voltage receptacle sat unused.

I started moving toward the utility area, but then a question popped into my head. "Why do you need a high-voltage plug?"

The delivery guy picked up the box and followed me. "It's for the recharging unit." He smiled, creating adorable little creases and dimples. He had model good looks. Perhaps this was his day job.

We went through the kitchen and I stood outside the alcove (next to the gas stove) and pointed at the empty plug. I didn't know how much that box weighed, but he just hefted it around like a feather pillow.

"Where do you want it?" he inquired and my mind started running erotic scenarios. Why couldn't he be the package instead of its deliverer?

"Um, what?" I had to pull myself back into reality. Placing one hand in front of my growing crotch probably did little to conceal my arousal.

"The recharging unit. You could either place it here," he indicated a space right outside the pantry, but that would make getting out the back door rather difficult. "Or we could move your machines around a bit to make room for it in there." He pointed into the alcove.

"Yeah, I like that better," I managed to mumble.

"Great." He smiled again, melting my resolve just a bit more. "Give me about five minutes and I'll have it all ready to go."

"Sure. I'll be… over there." I pointed to the breakfast nook overlooking the street. I could sit and finish my tea and try not to drool all over this guy.

I sat, sipping, gazing, cruising, listening to the noises coming from the kitchen. The scraping, bumping, rattling sounds stopped a few minutes later and the gorgeous guy walked up to me.

"All ready to go, Marques." His voice radiated calm and sensuality. Almost perfect.

"Uh, yeah." I stood, or, rather, attempted to stand, with a bit of a boner.

"Do you want to see it?" he asked with a smiling invitation.

The bit of a boner went to full staff. I tried to hide the bulge, but I could sense his eyes looking down at my crotch. He walked back to the kitchen and I followed with a bit of a limp.

In the crook of the utility area stood a clear, cylindrical thing that resembled a shower stall with a dome over it. "What's that?" I asked.

He walked into it and turned around. "It's my recharging unit. Does it fit okay?" He moved his hands around to indicate placement.

"*Your* recharging unit?" I nearly came in my pants. "You mean *you're* the guy?"

"Yes. I'm the guy." He pointed at himself then stuck out his hand to shake.

I stood frozen, transfixed. I faced paying off this gorgeous hunk like a mortgage? Well, well worth the money.

With trepidation, I extended my hand to him. He grasped it to shake. Not too tight, not too loose. My knees went weak. "Wow… not what I expected."

His lowered eyebrows expressed concern. "What was it you were expecting?"

I pointed to the empty cardboard box by the back door. "I thought you were going to be in that."

He laughed with a warmth that would have made me pee if I didn't have such a hard-on. I laughed along with him. We smiled at each other and I looked into his eyes, wondering what was behind them. He looked perfectly human and even smelled of slightly salty sweat.

When I recovered my senses, I asked, "What's your name? What do I call you?"

"What would you like to call me? I have no assigned name, just a model and serial number that might not make much sense to you."

As I looked at his endearing face, my mind ran through a bunch of potential candidates: Bill, Dave, Bruce, Howard, Paul, James. None of them seemed quite right. Then I thought about the service that provided him and came up with Manny. "What about Manny?"

His head moved a bit and he repeated "Manny" in his mellifluous tone. "If that is what you wish, Manny it is." He took a step closer and hugged me. I nearly exploded.

As much as I wanted to rip off his clothes and explore the rest of his body, we spent the remainder of the morning discussing logistics: how often he needs to recharge, what kind of nourishment he uses, all the minutiae of real life. Once I finished my tea, we walked down to the Castro area to shop for his own clothes. Even though he was the same size as me, I felt having him wearing my stuff seemed a bit too egotistical.

When we stopped for lunch, men walked by smiling at him. He was very attractive, after all. Guess I'm going to have to get used to that. He's probably not programmed for jealousy, but I certainly was.

Once we got back to my place with a dozen bags of new clothes, we dropped them on the floor of the bedroom and just stared at each other.

"Would you like to see me in a new outfit?" he asked as if inquiring about the price of butter.

I nodded, too enthralled with his appearance to speak. Once he started to unbutton his shirt, I could stand it no longer. Leaping across the bed, I tore at the offending fabric, ripping it, popping the buttons, but it didn't matter because he would no longer need that particular shirt. As I examined his physique at close range, I could not discern any edges or seams to the imitation skin. He even smelled manly. I found it truly remarkable.

"Marques"–I love hearing him say my name–"I can undress myself. Don't you want me to put on one of the new sets of clothing you bought me?" He picked up a shirt and pants, his quizzical look made him even more desirable.

My breathing came in heaves, and I could feel my palms moisten. "Manny, since I first saw you this morning, I have wanted to be totally naked with you. The whole shopping trip was like extended foreplay for me and now I must have what I want, what I've been waiting for." My eyes became tiger eyes. My haunches, lion haunches.

Manny dropped the new clothes to the floor and joined me on the bed, unbuttoning my shirt with care as he descended. Oh, my. His chest felt firm and ripply. My dick was steeled for action. Within a minute we were both naked. He looked just like a real human being.

Except that when I looked down at his crotch, I saw no equipment there. Nothing!

"Hey, where's your junk, Manny?"

He smiled. "We wait until the first sexual encounter to create our organs so that we can form them precisely the way you desire."

My mind raced with possibilities. This was even better than I had anticipated. I had not had sex in so long that I was afraid I might burst at any moment.

"How would you like me?" he inquired with unsophisticated innocence.

Two hours later I lay exhausted on the bed. I came three times and felt like a sweaty mess. The two of us hugged and looked at each other. This was exactly what I wanted for my sex life. Finally, a partner who knew what I liked and could give it to me just the way I wanted.

Manny lifted himself up, smiling at me. "Do you require a shower now, Marques?"

I'm sure I required a shower, but there was no energy left in my own power source. "In a while, Manny. Can we lay here for a bit longer?" I looked into his indecipherable eyes while I began my own recharge cycle.

"Of course, Marques. I want what you want." He smiled, re-assuring me.

This time, I think I got precisely what I wanted.

The next morning I woke to an empty bed. We had fallen asleep last night after watching the late news and another round of sex. When I got to the kitchen, Manny was in his recharging station, staring at me with a smile. It seemed a bit creepy until I began to think of it as a kind of shower stall he uses with his clothes on.

"Good morning, Marques. Did you sleep well?"

"Um, yes, I did, but I expected to wake up with you next to me. Just a bit of a surprise," I responded.

He stepped out of the utility alcove. "I waited until you fell asleep and then went into my recharging cycle. I did not want to wake you, and so I waited here until you arose."

"Oh," I said with a bit of disappointment.

Manny looked at me with concern. "Is that not pleasing to you, Marques? Should I do things differently?"

I guess he does have to recharge at some point, but I enjoy waking up next to the guy I fell asleep with. "It would be nice to wake up with you next to me, " I managed to utter with a bit too much violet-blue in my voice.

"I understand what you are saying, Marques. Tomorrow morning I shall get back in bed when I have finished recharging. Is that okay with you?"

Now it was my turn to smile. "Yes, oh, yes, oh, yes."

The phone rang. A woman calling from Manscapes wanted to know how the delivery went and if the unit was to my satisfaction. I gave exceptional feedback and praised their service. She told me I can get a break on my payments if I could get friends to use Manscapes as well. I thanked her for that information and thought about whether I even had any friends, and if I did have any friends, would I have been comfortable recommending this to them, and, finally, if I did have any friends I could recommend, would they have been able to afford it.

The next few months were like heaven on earth, if such a thing existed. Any time I had an issue with Manny or his behavior, I would bring it to his attention, and he would make adjustments to comply with my wishes. If only real men could reprogram themselves with such ease.

Any time I faced a difficult situation in my own life, I would discuss it with Manny. He helped me to realize that I had not been looking at all my available options before making decisions. One day, he told me that occasionally you can even come up with an unexpected result that works out better than you had ever anticipated.

Our life together brought me much joy and happiness. Every so often I had to consider whether the idea of having a relationship with an artificial person was a good idea, but when I weighed it against all of the problems I've had with other men, real men, I smiled and looked at my Manny.

I hadn't needed to mention it before, but my source of income came from arranging real estate loans for first-time buyers. As long as young couples needed new homes, I would be earning more money than I knew what to do with. Of course, now, a large chunk of that went to the cost of my constant companion, Manny. I couldn't imagine what life without him would be like.

But one day I had to imagine what life without him would be like. No one could have predicted the sudden collapse of the real estate market. Home sales halted almost immediately. Foreign economies faltered, stock markets slid, everyone panicked.

Without my regular income, I would no longer be able to afford Manny. Of course, I had some money put away for emergencies, but the payments to Manscapes went through my savings in a very short time.

A few months passed, but no one from the company contacted me about it. One evening I brought the issue up with Manny.

"I had noticed you stopped payment on my service," he said. "I hoped it was not because you were dissatisfied with me." He glanced down to the floor. So human in so many respects.

"No, no," I wanted to seem reassuring. "Of course, it's not you." I pointed at him. "Anytime I have ever brought up an issue, you quickly reprogram yourself, or whatever it is you do." Manny looked at me again with his probing gaze. "I have not been able to keep up my payments because of the sudden downturn in the economy." He smiled a little. Then it hit me, "How do you know whether I've paid my bill or not?"

"Oh, we are sent daily updates, and one of the things they keep us informed on is your payment record so that if there is a problem, we can resolve it, if possible." He sounded cold and logical in delivering that message. It seemed odd for once.

"I see," I said, feeling a distance from him for the very first time.

"In fact, Manscapes is coming to take me away tomorrow morning at nine o'clock."

"Tomorrow!?" I exclaimed. "That's not much notice."

"No, I guess it is not." If Manny were human, I would have to say he seemed ashamed. "I am going into my recharging unit now, and they will deactivate me. I am sorry, Marques." He walked to the kitchen.

"Wait!" I screamed after him. "Isn't there anything we can do? Didn't you teach me to always look for alternatives?"

Without pausing, he stepped into the recharging unit and turned around to face me. "We have exhausted all possible alternatives, Marques," sounding more like a recorded message than a spoken sentence. "Also, you tend to split infinitives."

His eyes closed. I went to him and tried to hug him, but there was no room in the recharging unit. His body stood immobile.

My tears commenced to stream.

The following morning I stood bleary-eyed in the kitchen with my morning tea, staring at Manny in his recharging unit with a slight bulge in my drawers. I did not want to wait by the front window and preferred to make the best of the last few moments with him. The chances of having another similar partner seemed infinitesimal, but at least I have had the experience of living with someone instead of prolonged dating that ends with an eventual grumble. Perhaps heterosexuals had a similar problem. Maybe it's men in general. Probably something to do with all that testosterone we have.

At precisely nine o'clock, the door buzzed. I took one last look at Manny, motionless, lifeless, deactivated. Instead of pressing the button at the top of the stairs, I walked down myself. I opened the door and screeched in delight.

"Manny! What are you doing here? I just left you upstairs. How'd you get down here so fast?"

He cocked his head a bit and then said, "Oh, I see the confusion. You must have the model that looks like me."

This guy resembled Manny in every regard. Even the voice sounded the same. "Sorry," I mumbled, somewhat embarrassed.

"No problem," he smiled that heart-melting smile I had grown to love. "We all look the same."

I opened the door farther and let him in. We walked up the stairs in silence. At the top, a flash went off in my head. If there's one thing I learned from Manny, it was to calculate all the options before making a final decision. Once in a while you can come up with an unexpected result. The two of us walked into the kitchen together.

"And there's *nothing* I could do to keep him?" I grasped at any possibility now. If only I could get inside Manny's adorable head and utilize that amazing power of calculation.

"You failed to adequately maintain your monthly payments, sir. You can't get something for nothing." He fiddled with the recharging unit.

"So… you look just like my model," using his word, "but can you access his memories?"

"Oh, sure. He was designed after me, and he sent daily reports and updates."

I studied this new fellow with an inquisitive angle. "Then you could download his information and become just like him?" I suggested.

He laughed that memorable laugh again, "And why would I want to do that?" Those dimples. "I'm here to essentially take him away." He turned back to the unit.

"Hold on," I ordered, and he paused. "I know I can't afford him now, but if, in the future, I have the funds again, I could get another Manny with the same memories and programming?"

"Yes, but…"

"So, there is hope after all," I said to myself.

"Anyway," the guy went on, "you're quite good-looking. I would expect you not to really have much trouble finding a regular man."

Perhaps my figure did improve a bit due to all the extra exercise I had gotten with Manny, and my clothes were starting to feel a bit loose. That made me smile a little. But, again, that did not help with the fact that all the other guys were duds.

We looked at each other for a bit longer than I expected. My dick began to grow again without an invitation. He glanced down at my pants and I moved my hands in front of my groin.

He grinned. "And you seem to also find me attractive, I see."

"My Manny was a dream lover. Sorry." I looked at the frozen figure again. "I don't believe I will ever find a real man like him." A small tear leaked down the side of my face.

"I finish at six. Would you like to get a drink or something to eat?"

Huh?? Was this *thing* asking me out? "Ummmm, you're allowed to have a social life? Don't you have to regenerate or something at night?"

He laughed so hard I thought he might bust a hairspring. "Oh, you thought..." he continued to chuckle, "I was..." I hoped he didn't require any emergency mechanical attention or repair. "No, I'm not like *him*." He pointed to Manny.

"I'm afraid I'm not following you. Are you, like, a newer model or something?"

Again he burst out in laughter. This was getting a little weird.

When he finally stopped guffawing, he extended his right hand. "I really like you…"

"Marques?" I offered.

"Marques." He took my hand and shook it. "I'm Sven."

"Sven?"

"Yes, Sven." His smile calmed me back down. "This unit," he pointed at Manny, "was modeled after me. Apparently, a lot of guys find me attractive."

Now that I noticed it, his sweat smelled distinctly different. My jaw gave in to gravity and fell. "You mean you're not a… a…" I pointed at Manny.

"No." He pulled his hand back. "Human, like you. I assume." He appeared to be studying me for access ports.

"Yes, I am all too human, I'm afraid." I had difficulty believing this fluky situation.

He stopped checking my body and smiled. "If you help me get this unit out of here, maybe we can go grab a quick cup of coffee together before I have to eventually get to my next appointment."

So, there was a real guy like Manny, after all. I was about to tell him I didn't drink coffee and that he tends to split infinitives, but then the logic of doing that did not make sense. "Sure," I managed to squeak out, "that would be great!"

Welcome to ViReLand

One of the many journals asked for stories involving fluid sexuality in a speculative fiction setting. This is my attempt (which did not make it into the published collection). As we spend more and more of our free time online with more sophisticated gadgets, I can only imagine one day, we will have such a diversion available.

Welcome to ViReLand

The title flashed and floated in front of my eyes.

ViReLand

Big, bold, bright letters captivated my attention.

Touch here to continue.

From within the virtual reality interface I raised a finger to the colorful text.

Welcome to ViReLand, the ultimate Virtual Reality experience.

The welcoming message hovered above a greenish background. It took a few moments to adapt to the sensation of seeing through the eyepieces. Perhaps it was my imagination, but I thought I smelled flowers.

The scene changed to an idyllic park with a pond and some benches around it, but it wasn't totally in focus.

Type detected. Language detected. Touch here to enter.

It had taken me almost two years of extra work hours to save up for the interface and the online subscription. ViReLand had revolutionized our world from the time its first version appeared about five years ago. Almost everyone I knew who could afford it was linked in and spent much of their free time here. In fact, most of their social engagements occurred online now, and this global service has allowed family members and old friends to keep in touch much more than was possible before. If only it didn't cost so much, but I'm about to find out what makes it worth the price.

When I touched the floating text, it disappeared and the scene beyond resolved into focus. Around the pond I could see others, mostly involved in sex rings of three to about ten. The sounds of pleasure almost overshadowed the experience, but they all seemed to be enjoying themselves. One group of three people managed to balance precariously on one of the benches as they engaged in their activity. Personally, I prefer smaller groups because, well, it's a bit embarrassing, but my left sex organ is oddly small and my right sex organ is above-average in size. This makes linking into sex rings difficult because I have to find others whose sex organs match mine, and that has not been easy. In fact, one of the reasons I have sought out this virtual experience was so that I can engage in normal sex rings without having to deal with my differently-sized sex organs.

I approached one of the groups of three by the water and tapped the back of one of the people to request an opening for linking. Without saying a thing, two people detached and invited me in. Wow! This was so much easier than in real life!

Just as I prepared to attach to the others, I looked down and realized that my left sex organ was on the right, and the right sex organ on the left! This was not going to work. The two people who had detached then turned to look at what caused the delay. One started laughing and the other proclaimed loudly, "Get out of here, you freak! Go engage with your own kind!" and they rejoined, pushing me away.

How could this happen? My virtual reality avatar was also mis-shapen. There must be a way to change a setting or something. While I contemplated my situation, another undulating ring bumped into me, knocking me to the ground. I stood up and moved off to the Menu portal visible near a large shrub.

When I stepped through, the scenery went out of focus again and I could see a list of choices. I chose *Settings*, hoping to find a way to revise my errant sex organs so that they would be in their proper orientation.

Hundreds of options allowed the user to change height, color, type, and so forth, but no listing for sexual organs. How frustrating! Back at the main menu, I chose *Exit*. The door appeared and I passed through, leaving the simulation.

What an amazing experience! In ViReLand I could see, touch, smell and hear everything so clearly, but somehow my sex organs got reversed, making it impossible, or virtually impossible, to satisfy my intensifying drive.

I looked online for information about the simulation, and nothing addressed my particular situation. I've already produced three offspring in real life. If I accidentally reproduce again, I'd go over the legal limit and might have to spend the rest of my days in prison.

This has had to happen to someone else, so I told myself I would contact the game's manufacturer tomorrow. It was getting late, and I had much to do at work.

The next day I contacted the ViReLand support staff. How frustrating to have to go through so many levels of menus and choices before getting to actually speak with someone. And then, when I did get connected, the person spoke with an unfamiliar accent, making it difficult to understand. I kept trying to explain my situation, but the response I kept getting was, "Have you rebooted your system? I want to assist, but we cannot help you until you reboot your system."

That evening, I rebooted the system and tried re-entering ViReLand again after getting into the interface. After passing through the opening entryway, I stood once again near the pond watching others engaged in sex rings. Before I made the same mistake again, I looked down to examine my sex organs. Darn! The left was on the right and vice versa again! What can I do?

There must be someplace where I can go and ask other users about this. I followed a path that led out of the wooded area and into a more urban setting. Tall buildings lined the background, and I stood at the intersection of two residential streets. People walked past, some alone, some with others engaged in conversation. No one looked at me as they went on their own business.

For about an hour I wandered around, exploring the new surroundings. I could see advertising for new products and services. Signs with changing messages and alerts. Perhaps in time I would find out how to get something posted up there that might help me along.

My biggest fear was that I would run into someone I know, someone I work with, or, the worst possible thing, my boss. Then again, I might not look like my regular self, and they might not either. A store window reflected light and I walked up to it so that I could get a look at my avatar. Oh, my! This simulation made me look really good, at least to me that is. The face was somewhat similar, but just slightly different so that a friend, co-worker, or boss, would not recognize me immediately. The body shape was much trimmer, however. But when I started taking a closer look at the others, I began to realize that we all looked fairly alike in shape and size. The only real differences appeared to be colorations of eyes, hair, and skin.

I guess the program's character generator was somewhat limited in scope. If everyone looked nearly the same, how are we to tell each other apart? Perhaps that was part of the game design.

On the wall next to the window was a Menu portal and I walked through it. The scene went fuzzy and an information screen appeared. According to the system, I would need to eat soon, replenishing my energy, and I also needed to choose a career path. As my regular job was in the medical field, I should probably pick something unrelated. The choices were: Education, Entertainment, Finance, Hospitality, Medical, Science, and Service. Having already been a teacher following my higher education, being somewhat shy, knowing nothing about finance, hated waiting tables during my higher education, skipping my own profession, and having a dislike for scientific studies (despite my medical degree), I settled on Service, whatever that might be.

When I touched that menu selection, a group of subcategories appeared: Administrative, Military, Personal, Social Work, and Spiritual. The idea of being someone else's personal servant sounded repulsive, but I would imagine the setting would be nice. I touched that.

The menu disappeared, the scene returned to normal, and through the archway, I saw a large limousine pulling up to the curb. The rear door opened, and someone inside beckoned me to enter. Intrigue! At last, the adventure began.

Figuring I had nothing to lose, I crouched down into the limo. When the door closed automatically behind me I got a bit nervous, but then realized this was all a simulation and fear of pain or anguish was groundless. An icon that looked like food flashed rapidly in front of my face, and I touched it. The flashing slowed somewhat and I touched it again. This time, not only did the rate of flashing decrease, but the color changed a bit as well. I kept touching the icon until the flashing stopped completely and the color stayed constant. I guess I'm not hungry anymore!

While I was busy "feeding" myself, the scenery out the windows changed gradually from urban to rural. At the top of a lone hill I could see what looked like a large, gothic mansion keeping watch over the world below. The car kept getting closer to it, and eventually we pulled onto the road that presumably wound its way up to the huge home at the top of the hill.

Looks like I'll be providing "Personal Services" for whoever lived in that isolated mansion. Even if the work was not to my liking, the scenery and views promised to be spectacular.

When the car stopped, the door opened automatically, and a well-dressed person in an old-style, vintage suit stood there watching me exit. My first impulse was to look all around. Even though I knew this was a computer simulation, it was difficult to believe that the scenery wasn't real. I could see the town below where I had started, and the little park. The house looked like something out of a story from about 100 years ago. This was going to be awesome!

"I am Toff. Follow me," came the command. Toff turned and walked off and I followed. The front entryway of the home dissolved as we approached, and the two of us stepped inside. When I turned back to look, that part of the wall reappeared. Amazing!

The inside looked like a museum of bad taste. Oddly-colored pieces of uncomfortable-looking furniture sat amidst unattractive bits of statues and art pieces. Musty-smelling air added to the sensation of being in an antique venue. Several stairways led away from the main room in different directions, and I could see a manicured yard through the picture window at the rear.

"This way, please," Toff commanded from the top of one of the various stairways. I hoped I could learn the geography and topography of this place quickly enough. I descended, and at a doorway along the corridor at the bottom of the stairs, Toff pointed into a room. "This will be your quarters. Return to the main room for a briefing when you have acquainted yourself."

I stepped cautiously into the new room and saw four narrow beds neatly arranged, looking like they'd never been slept in and would never be used. When I turned back to thank Toff, all I saw was the hallway wall opposite the door. Oh well, I would be going to 'orientation' or 'briefing' or 'whatever' soon enough.

As I surveyed the small room, the door opened and a very attractive person wearing that same vintage clothing entered. I looked down at myself and realized I now wore a similar suit.

"Oh, hello! You must be one of the new ones. I'm Yelto," and we greeted each other. "Are you ready to go to the briefing?"

At least one person was friendly here. I was beginning to wonder if they were all like Toff, business-like and emotionless.

"I think Toff is waiting for us upstairs."

"Are you another player or are you part of the simulation?" I had to ask.

Yelto laughed shyly, "I'm a real person, just like you. Toff is part of the simulation, but you get used to that fairly quickly. Let's go."

I had no idea what this Yelto looked like in real life, but I found the avatar rather appealing, even though the body shape was fairly similar to mine. Perhaps the color choices aroused my curiosity. I could sense one of my sex organs beginning to respond to the attraction.

We walked up the stairs, and Yelto managed to occupy one of the ridiculous pieces of furniture. I decided to stand. No matter how long the 'briefing' would be, it seemed standing would ultimately be more comfortable.

A few others, also attired in period clothing, sat or stood, and Toff waited until we all were ready. "You have all chosen a career of Personal Service. My name is Toff, and I will be your supervisor for this stage of advancement. Welcome to Lommy House."

Lommy. Now there's a term I have not heard in a long time. In fact, I think it came out of my own mouth when I wanted to make fun of a schoolmate years before. Not a nice word, but now I suppose I must give it a second thought.

"Here at Lommy House," Toff continued, "we accommodate those of you who are different. Look around. You will see that the system has presented each of you with some sort of challenge, making it difficult to assimilate into everyday life."

Toff paused and we all looked at each other and ourselves, discovering our own differences. A few others had sex organ arrangements like me. One person had two left sex organs and three people had two right ones. And I thought I had it bad! Now I understood their use of the word, 'Lommy.'

"We respect all of your differences at Lommy House, and we expect you to have the same respect for others as you work and learn under my supervision. If you do not feel you are capable of living under these circumstances, we invite you to leave now." Toff indicated the front entryway, which disintegrated again. One of the people with reversed sex organs like me stood up and walked out. It seemed a bit odd for someone like that to be so intolerant of others. After that person left, the wall reappeared again.

Toff peered at each of us in turn. "I am glad that you have remained. I have one more choice for you all to make." The back picture window that displayed the garden beyond fluttered, and two openings appeared. Floral fragrances wafted in. Toff walked toward the garden, stopped, and turned back to us.

"You see here two entrances to the garden. We will convene there in a minute or so after each of you has made yet another decision." Toff indicated a door on the left. "This is the way out to the garden. If you pass through here, you end up behind me, in the garden." With a nod to the door on the right, "However, if you choose this one, you will end up at the front of Lommy House and the limousine will transport you back to town. And, you will also find that whatever differences, challenges or difficulties you have been presented with will be reversed, cured, or resolved."

We all looked at each other questioningly. What does this mean? We can get rid of our abnormalities and participate fully in ViReLand?

One of the others spoke, "If we choose to leave now, can we come back later?"

Toff looked sternly at the questioner, "No. This decision is final. Once you pass through the door to the outside, you will never be allowed to return to Lommy House."

"What do you think we should do?" Yelto turned to me for advice. My other sex organ began to respond in an untimely fashion.

Others discussed this decision as well.

"I'm not sure I know what I want to do." I responded. "I tried looking in the Settings menus for some way to take care of this but couldn't find anything helpful. What do you think?"

Just as Yelto was about to speak, the scene went blurry and a message appeared:

Time for sleep. Touch here to pause.

I did not realize this program had a built-in reminder that real life continued while we were away. Yes, I had to work in the morning, and perhaps this would give me more time to ponder the question as to which door to choose.

When I tapped the message, the visual went dark, and I began to remove the interface. I had forgotten to eat, but I could probably stand to lose a bit of weight anyway. I headed off to bed craving both food and guidance.

All the next day at work I had the decision in the back of my mind as to which door to choose, which made it difficult to concentrate on my job. I could solve my sex organ difficulty and participate in all the sex rings I had seen, or I could accept the differences and attempt to live with those particular challenges. The whole idea of virtual reality, as I understood it, was to experience things you wouldn't normally get to do in real life. But who would choose to live an outsider's life, full of difficulties to overcome?

Oh, ViReLand, you tempt me. Do I take the easy path and just have fun or do I make the hard choice and discover what life is like for people who might be different?

That evening I ate a light meal before re-attaching the interface, just in case I ended up exhausting my time again. Once prepared, the system returned me to the main room of the Lommy

House. I could see out into the florid garden, where most of the people I recognized, including Yelto and Toff, stood talking.

So here I am. One door leads to a normal, happy, sex-filled life with many new and wonderful experiences. The other door leads to potential frustrations and various challenges to surmount. Each choice had its pluses and minuses, pros and cons, benefits and disadvantages.

I stand looking out at the seemingly-content group wondering what it would be like. Of course, I had to realize and accept that I already face real-life challenges with my own disfigured sex organs.

Oh, ViReLand!

Yelto sees me standing, smiles, and waves for me to join the group in the garden.

Closest to the Jack

Written for a collection of stories about older gay relationships, this story did not make the cut. I've always enjoyed playing bocce, and it seemed like a great metaphor for so many things.

Closest to the Jack

Every Tuesday at 2:30, Paolo and Giacomo meet for bocce at the courts in City Park. Paolo prefers the lane far at the end. He does not like being boxed in by other people, especially those young show-offs with mock versions of their authentic caps and the paper cups of watered-down cappuccino.

Now that it is 2:45 and Giacomo has yet to show up, Paolo starts to get worried something happened to his friend of fifty years. He looks at the path leading to the bocce courts, but no one seems to be approaching.

Oh, well, not today, vecchio mio.

He picks up his set of balls and stands, looking one last time for his friend.

"Are you Paolo?" he hears from behind. A man's voice, not a young man, but one with the same accent he and Giacomo brought with them from the Old Country.

When he turns about, he sees a slightly younger version of his Giacomo. A bit thinner, a bit more hair, a bit less grey, but not much.

"I am Paolo. And you are…?"

"Giuseppe, Jack's brother."

How can you know someone fifty years and never hear about a brother?

"Is he all right? We play bocce every Tuesday afternoon."

"Yes," Giuseppe nods, "He is fine. Something came up and he could not meet you today. I came here to let you know."

"*Grazie.* I guess I can go home now." Paolo starts to walk away.

"Wait! I also came to play in his place." Paolo stops. "If you want to, that is."

Fuori di testa. *Do I really want to break in a new partner now?*

"Can you even play bocce?" Paolo asks irritably.

Giuseppe laughs in short bursts, similar to his brother. "Of course I can play bocce. Didn't Jack tell you?"

"*Un bel niente, amico,*" Paolo blurts. "Giacomo never even mentioned he has a brother, and we have known each other since grade school." He puts his flattened palm down to his side to indicate a child's height.

Again, Giuseppe laughs, which is starting to irritate Paolo further. "That is just like him. I don't think he ever tells anyone about me."

"As a matter of fact, I've never heard anyone call him Jack before. It's always been Giacomo."

"Really?" Giuseppe's eyebrows elevate sharply. "I've only ever called him Jack."

"Maybe we are speaking of a different person. Perhaps your brother is not the one I play bocce with after all. *Addio.*" He tosses his free hand skyward and starts off again.

"Wait." Paolo stops and turns back. "I know this may sound a bit odd, but Jack had his reasons for not telling you about me."

With the eye of a butcher examining a side of beef for the best place to begin chopping, Paolo looks at Giuseppe more closely. "*Per favore*, give me an example."

The younger man looks up at the trees surrounding the courts. "Well, first off, he is extremely jealous of my bocce playing. I win tournaments he cannot play in."

Paolo scrutinizes the other fellow and notices he had brought a case with balls as well. "I see you have your own set. Is it more special than the one he and I have used for years?"

"I'm not sure. Bring it here and let me see it."

Vaffanculo! *I should have to go to him? I am the old man here.*

Paolo treads back to the spot next to Giuseppe and opens the time-worn sack with the four red, four green, and one white ball. The scratches and divots suggest a well-used set, yet one that still functions.

"You guys use a plastic Jack?" Giuseppe seems surprised.

"A plastic what?"

"The Jack." He points to the smaller white ball.

"That's the *Pallino*. Who calls it a Jack?"

Again with the laugh. "I guess *I* do."

"And what do *you* use, Mr. Tournament Winner?"

Giuseppe picks up the leather-bound carrying case he had set carefully on the ground. "I'll show you." He flips up the latches and opens the lid to reveal four bright blue, four day-glow orange, and one smaller steel sphere. The larger balls are shiny, lacquered, polished.

Sunlight reflects off the metal Jack directly into Paolo's eyes. He drops his satchel and raises an arm reflexively to block the onslaught.

Scemo! *He is trying to kill me.*

"Sorry," Giuseppe exclaims. "I usually play indoors."

Indoors? Who plays indoors? Bocce is lawn bowling. Lawns are outside. Where is my Giacomo? Why isn't he here?

"Also, I haven't been around much lately. I came to visit with Jack for a few weeks while my penthouse is being renovated."

A penthouse? How richy-rich can this guy be? Paolo stares at him with a bit of the butcher's eye again.

"Well, all right. That's only part of it," Giuseppe divulges. "Jack has never been able to accept some things about who I am and how I have led my life." He looks away. "Also, my boyfriend of eleven years walked out last week and I needed to get away for a while." A sniffle.

Oh, finocchio. *That explains it.*

"And," Giuseppe adds, "there is another reason why Jack asked me to meet you here today."

Paolo's ears perk up. Perhaps there is something worth waiting for here.

"But maybe we should play a bit first—to get acquainted." He tosses the metal ball down the lane.

Paolo stands eyeing the strange object on his territory. He turns to Giuseppe, "How about if we use our old-fashioned *palle.*" He kneels to his beat-up canvas bag and picks up one of the red balls. After another scrutinizing glance at the young upstart, Paolo steps to the line and looks out at the unfamiliar sphere.

I will teach this one a lesson.

He crouches into his bowling position and tosses the splintery ball into the lane. It rolls slowly out toward the little steel ball and stops about a centimeter beyond it.

There, beat that, allocco.

Paolo reaches down into his case again and picks up two of the green balls. "*Tocca a te*–it's up to you, your turn." He presents them to Giuseppe.

The younger man smiles and studies his opponent's face. He nods, takes just one ball and steps to the line. Giuseppe weighs it with his hand, executes a slight flourish, a twist of the wrist, and launches the ball. It hits the ground about a meter out and swings to the right, almost touching the wall but not quite. Like a circular boomerang, it curves around the Jack and rolls up to the red ball already there, nudging it a few centimeters away.

Paolo stands gaping at this feat.

Giuseppe smiles impishly. "I told you I've won a few tournaments."

"Where did you learn how to do that?"

The marble white skin of Giuseppe's face reddens. "Jack taught me everything I know about bocce."

I have never seen Giacomo do that. Well, I have a few tricks up my sleeve as well.

Standing at the line with the second red ball, Paolo looks over at the newcomer again before bowling.

He looks even more like Dean Martin than his brother. Che cacasodo bello.

With balletic grace, the red ball dances down the lane, careening off the green one, moving it away from the target.

"Very nice!" Giuseppe compliments. "I can see why my brother likes to have you as an opponent." He takes the second green ball and studies the lay. His roll is long, leaving Paolo's ball closer to the Jack. When he turns to take the third ball, their eyes meet for the first time, and the contact lasts for a few seconds longer than might be comfortable for the older man.

Giuseppe takes the ball, smiles, and steps to the line. In a fanfare of wrist gyration, he launches the green sphere on its way. It passes most of the other balls but bounces off the last one he threw, reflecting it backwards, coming to rest up against the steel ball.

Oh, strategic, this one!

Paolo nods slowly with his lower lip protruding. He picks up his third red ball and stands at the line contemplating. After fifteen seconds or so, and another glance at the handsome *pezzo*, he crouches down, swings back, and bowls. This one heads directly for the last ball Giuseppe threw, knocking it away, leaving his red one in its place. With a smirk, he glances over at his competitor.

The younger man shakes his head, slightly bowed, and picks up the last green ball.

"Hold on," Paolo interrupts. Giuseppe looks at him. "Before you roll your last, I want to know why Giacomo sent you today."

"You don't…," he pauses, "do you?" Giuseppe poses. "My brother has known for several years about you, but he never said anything because you guys are such good friends and you have never, ever, made him feel uncomfortable."

What could he be talking about? Uncomfortable?

The younger fellow observes Paolo. "I can tell you are puzzled. Perhaps this is something you haven't even realized yourself." He walks to the line. "Jack catches the way you look at him. At first he was scared, but then recognized the innocence of your attraction."

Attraction? He thinks I am finocchio *too? Quite the* cazzo arrapato.

"And I find you *molto bello* as well. Can we go for espresso somewhere after this?" He turns back to the lane and sends the last green ball speeding toward the assortment of others. It smacks into the Jack, sending it off toward the back, right next to one of the other green balls.

With a nod of his head, Giuseppe whispers, "*Tocca a te,* Paolo."

Rumpspringa

Written as a call for submission for stories where the sense of "place" was most important, this and the title story ("Looking for Love in All the Right Places") never got sent because the journal cancelled the volume before the deadline.

Rumpspringa

Gary had never seen the likes of the boy who just walked into Mixer, one of the more recent bars to open in Chelsea. He had a farm-hewn look, like he just stepped down from a tractor clenching a dried stalk of wheat grass between his teeth.

Something about this stranger seemed intriguing, inviting, alluring. So out-of-place in this ultra-modern wash of dark walls, neon strip lights and fake smoke. The designer had set up the entrance so that each person walking in would emerge into the main room from a cloud of fog, like walking out of a dream.

And this seemed much like a dream to Gary. A hayseed hick in a flashy lower Manhattan gay bar. The kind of thing he used to watch at home on video late at night when he couldn't make a good connection at the bar. Just like in the dream, or video, the bucolic lad walked up to him.

"Hello, I'm Elmo," the farm boy thrust out his rough-looking right hand, presumably to shake with Gary. Unfortunately, the surprisingly-different name sent him into a giggle fit. "Did I say something wrong? I'm awfully sorry if I did. Perhaps I should just leave now." Elmo turned to go.

"No, wait, Elmo," Gary managed to blurt out before he started laughing again, almost spilling the pricey drink he had fought the jaded crowd to purchase. The liquid in the glass glowed blue in the light of the plexiglass bartop. "Can I buy you a drink? Are you even old enough to be in here?"

The farm boy had a very fresh and youthful appearance, except for the roughness of his palms. Elmo gazed down into those work-worn hands before responding, "I am not in the habit of accepting charity from strangers, but," and he glanced up at Gary's shirt and then his face, "I believe I am prepared to try something new to-night. Oh, and yes, I just turned 21 last week. What are you drinking, sir?"

"A Blue Moon," Gary responded as he pointed his free hand at the glass. "Two things"–he held up two fingers–"First off, this is not a drink for rank beginners, and two, if you call me 'sir' again, the deal's off." Elmo looked down. "Hey, up here, man. My name is Gary."

Elmo looked up and smiled. "Thank you… Gary."

And Gary returned the smile. Possible fantasy scenarios began to form in his overcharged imagination. "Do you like beer?"

"Of course!" Elmo's smile widened. "We have all kinds of beer at home: Apple Beer, Ginger Beer, Root Beer –"

"Do any of them have alcohol?" Gary interrupted.

"Oh, no," his moppy head shook side to side, "we're not sup-posed to drink alcohol."

"But you do, Elmo, don't you?"

A wicked smile spread across his face, "Oh, yeah, sure, but please don't tell my pa."

Gary gently grasped Elmo's arm. "Don't you worry yourself none, Elmo, your secret is safe with me." He then turned to the bartender and ordered a lite beer. Once he had finished settling, he took the bottle in his free hand and turned back to Elmo. "I wish we could find a place to sit and chat, but this bar is so crowded."

"What about there?" Elmo pointed to a café table where two nattily-dressed men had just stood up.

"Well, aren't you my little lucky charm, Elmo." He guided them to the recently-abandoned seats. "So… what brings a nice young boy like you into a filthy old place like this?" Once he had set the two drinks on the table, he waved his arms around to indicate the space.

"Oh, no. This is far from filthy. If you want filthy, I can show you the cow stalls." Elmo's head rotated around as he took in the new surroundings. "And why did you start laughing when I told you my name?" He confronted Gary directly.

"Oh"–he smiled–"it's not a name you hear very often. The only Elmo I ever knew was the one on Sesame Street."

"Is that far from here? Is it in Manhattan?"

Gary burst out laughing. "Are you for reals? Or are you just pranking me?"

"I'm not sure I understand what you are asking me, sir–Gary." His wide eyes suggested his innocence to be sincere. "Where I live, there are quite a few of us–Elmos, that is. In fact, folks usually call me Elmo Number 2, or just Number 2 for short."

"You are just full of surprises, Elmo Number 2." Gary grinned. "At first I had to suppress the urge to tickle you all over." He wiggled his fingers and moved his hands up and down.

"Why would you want to do that?" Elmo sipped at the beer.

"Well, a few years back there was this toy that… oh, never mind." Elmo seemed focused on Gary's shirt. "Is there something wrong with my shirt? You keep looking at it."

"Oh, no." He blushed. "It's the color. It's what drew me to you."

"Blue. Blue is what made you bee line from the door up to me and tell me your name?" Elmo nodded his head. "Think you could you help me out with a bit of an explanation?"

"Oh, sure," he took another sip of the beer, "And thank you for this. It's not bad. You see, at home, that shade of blue has a special significance for us."

"Home?" Gary gave him the once over once again. "And where might that be, Elmo?"

"Lancaster, of course!"

"Of course. I should have known. And you pronounce it way different from what I am used to. We say *Lan*-caster, but you call it '*Lank*-a-ster.'"

"Really? I've never heard it pronounced any other way."

"Uhn huhn," Gary started searching out other faces, just in case this cute little fantasy disappeared into a dust cloud. "So… what brings you to New York, Elmo Number 2?"

The farm boy giggled, "Number 2. It sounds so different when you say it." He giggled again. Perhaps it was the beer kicking in. "I'm on Rumspringa. Are you familiar with that?"

"Is it some new drug?" Gary stared down into his drink.

"Oh, no, silly. It's my time to discover what the outside world has to offer before I commit to my adult life."

"I think I saw a movie about that. Are you Amish or something?"

"Sort of. We like to call ourselves Pennsylvania Dutch, but it's very similar. My folks are more modern than some of the other groups."

"Obviously."

"Obviously?"

"Don't you people ride around in horse buggies? No electricity, no cell phones."

"Oh, that's the older ones. We're not so strict like that anymore."

"I see," Gary's eyes wandered over Elmo's body anew as fantasies began to redevelop. "So… you're in New York to see the sights?"

"That's tomorrow. I'm taking a big bus tour. It should be fun!"

"And tonight you're checking out gay bars?"

Elmo's head dropped. "Well, yeah, I guess you could say that."

"Your folks know you're gay?"

"They might. Don't know. I think they might have figured it out when I didn't choose any of the girls in town. They're hoping this trip might get that out of my system."

"Well, good luck with that, Brother Elmo." Gary started to stand up. The fantasies came to a non-grinding halt.

"Wait! Where are you going?"

Gary rolled his eyes and fluttered his lashes. "Elmo, you could say this is getting a bit much for me. Enjoy your stay. Follow your dreams."

"But, Gary, I thought you wanted to make love to me?"

He swung back. "Make what to who? What in the sweet name of Jesus are you talking about?"

"I thought we had some kind of connection and you would want to… well, you know…"

Maybe Gary's fantasies could be satisfied after all. It had been a while for him, and this roll in the hay could be just what he needed. At least he wouldn't have to work too hard to get the guy into bed. "Have you ever been with another man, Elmo?"

His face reddened. "Men, no… but plenty of boys. When we were younger we would all take care of each other's needs out behind the big barn. 'Practicing,' we called it. But then my friends all started taking a liking to girls, and I was the only one who didn't feel that way."

Another fantasy scene Gary could imagine. "Uhn huhn. Why don't you finish your beer and we'll take a walk together."

Elmo sucked the rest of the bottle in one gulp, banged it on the table, smiling, "I'm ready!" He launched off the stool and started toward the door.

Gary grabbed his shoulder, "Slow down there, cowboy. We haven't discussed where we're going."

"Oh, sorry. I just figured you'd walk me back to where I'm staying."

"And just where might that be, Elmo Number 2?"

"I'm staying in a hostel a few blocks away."

"I see." More fantasies. "Okay, let's book."

"Book? You like to read? That's great."

"Oh, brother." He grasped Elmo's hand, "Let's get out of here." Gary guided them through the door. "Which way?" Elmo gave him the address of the hostel. "That's on the way to my place. How convenient."

As they walked up the Avenue, Gary began to feel unnerved.

"Is something wrong, Gary?"

"Sshh, I think we are being followed."

Elmo turned to look back.

"No, don't –" Gary started.

"Good evening, gentlemen," came from one of two looming figures dressed in dark hoodies. "Enjoying your little stroll?"

"C'mon, Elmo, let's get out of here."

"Elmo?" The taller one laughed. "Your name is Elmo?"

"Yes, sir" he responded. "What of it?"

"Funny name. Now give me all your cash, your cell phones and any jewelry you might have and we'll call it a night, okay? Nobody needs to get hurt." The two ominous figures circled Gary and Elmo.

"Excuse me," Elmo offered, "I have no intentions of giving you any of my money."

"Oh, really?" the shorter one asked as he smacked a fist repeatedly into his palm.

"Just give them your stuff, Elmo. Don't make a scene."

"Elmo…" the shorter one laughed.

Before either of the would-be thieves could respond, Elmo pounded each of their faces with a balled up fist. Hard.

"Ow! Fucking sissies!" The taller one cried out.

"Come on, Gary! Run!"

The two young men sprinted off, turned a corner and halted to catch their breath.

"Number 2, you are my hero," Gary panted. "Where did you learn to do that?"

Elmo smiled. "Just one of the other things we practiced out behind the big barn. And please don't tell my pa. He does not condone violence."

Gary smiled and shook his head, "My friend, you are certainly full of surprises." He grasped Elmo's hand, and the two walked along the street in silence for a few minutes.

"Here's my hostel." Elmo pointed at the building they had stopped in front of. "Good night, and thanks again for the beer."

"Now just a minute here. I thought we were going to spend some more time together." Gary had to rearrange the growing business in his pants.

"We will. Just not on the first date, Gary. Tomorrow. Meet me here at 6 o'clock and we can go to dinner and chat some more."

"Now hold on. If all we're going to do is have dinner and chat, I don't think I want to be here at all."

Elmo smiled, "Well, that's where we'll start. Who knows where we'll end." He stepped up to Gary, hugged him tightly and planted a wet, smoochy kiss that lasted about ten seconds. "Good night. See you tomorrow. Hope you get home safely."

Gary did not have far to walk, and he certainly had enough fantasy material to keep him occupied for the night. The front of Elmo's trousers felt very hard and very large.

Being late to everything was Gary's way. 'On time' was not a phrase you might use in the same sentence with his name. However, the next day, following his editor shift at the magazine, he cleaned up and arrived at the hostel where Elmo stayed at 5:55.

The door opened and out walked Elmo with a grand smile. "So nice to see you're here on time. I value punctuality."

"Ummmm, don't get too used to it. Not my strong suit, you might say. So… tell me about your day. What did you see?"

Elmo described a tourist's dream of being shuttled around Manhattan all day and seeing all the sights he had heard about.

"That's amazing," Gary said. "I can't think of one place I would add to that list. Sounds like you've seen it all. You can die happy now."

"But I don't want to die now. I just met you."

Gary pulled Elmo in for a hug. "Number 2, you are *so* cute."

"Thanks, but I am also a bit hungry. We didn't stop much for food. Where would you suggest?"

"Do you like pizza?"

Elmo's face contorted a bit.

"Have you never had a pizza?"

"I'm not sure what you are asking me. A piece of what?"

Gary laughed. "Follow me." The two walked hand-in-hand to his favorite neighborhood pizzeria.

Once they sat down at the only table left, a middle-aged woman with an obvious wig came up to the table. "Your usual, Gary?" She looked down at Elmo, "And who's your little friend?"

"This is Elmo. Elmo meet Pauline."

"Hello, ma'am."

"Oh, polite, ain't he?" She gave him a second look. "Where'd you find him, Gary? Hang on to him. He's a keeper, I'm tellin' ya."

"Thanks, Pauline. So far, so good. Believe it or not –"

"And I don't," she interrupted and guffawed.

"Believe it or not, Miss Smartypants, he came up to me at Mixer last night."

"Well, nobody's perfect. Nice to meet you, Elmo. I'll put your order in. You guys want something to drink?"

"Better make it a large tonight. We're both kind of hungry. And two draft beers, please."

"Coming right up." She started walking to the kitchen, stopped and turned back to look at Gary. "Please? You said 'please'? He's definitely a keeper." Pauline then continued off.

Gary smiled at Elmo. "She sure likes you. And she's not one to hand out compliments freely, if you know what I mean."

"I think I do, Gary. She seems very… concerned for you." He smiled at Gary and reached out to grasp his hand.

"Now, if you two lovebirds would move your freakin' elbows, I can put the beers on the table." The men sat back, and Pauline set two large frosty glass mugs down. Elmo looked up at her and she winked before heading back to the kitchen.

"Gary, that woman just winked at me! Is she interested in me?"

Gary laughed. "No, Elmo. That's just her way of letting you know she thinks you're a nice person."

"I am a nice person."

"Yes. Yes, you are." He smiled again.

While they waited for the pizza to arrive, Gary told about how he grew up in Oyster Bay, studied English at Columbia, and went into publishing. Elmo explained farm life: the chores, the schedule, the expectations.

"Make way, fellas." Pauline appeared out of nowhere with a huge pizza. "*Mangia*," she admonished as she walked away.

"What did she say?" Elmo asked.

"It means 'eat' in Italian."

"Is she Italian?"

Gary shook his head. "Just eat."

Elmo observed Gary's ritual of taking a piece, dabbing the top with a napkin, creasing it between the thumb and first two fingers, and finally eating it. His first attempt was a bit clumsy, but he did manage to get part of the pointy end into his mouth before it flopped down.

"Well?" Gary inquired.

"Hey! This is good!"

Elmo continued explaining how his father expects him to take over the dairy farm when he retires, just the way his father took it from his grandfather, and so forth, back over 100 years.

"Wow! Your family has run a dairy for 100 years? Nothing around here ever lasts that long."

"I don't mean to be rude," Elmo looked at Gary, "but from what our tour guide said today, both the bridge to Brooklyn and the Statue of Liberty are both over 100 years old." He shoveled another slice into his mouth, now that he had the routine down.

"Yes, you are right, Number 2. You're a fast learner."

At the end of the meal, Gary picked up the check and said, "Don't worry. This time it's on me, but next time, we'll have to renegotiate."

"Sure, Gary. Sure."

They both stood and walked toward the door.

"Goodnight, fellas." Pauline roared from the back. "Keep it clean, now."

"What did she mean about keeping it clean? And what is it we have to clean? Were we supposed to take care of the dishes?"

"Oh, Elmo." Gary rubbed the top of his friend's head. "You are *so* darn cute."

"Thanks. You too." And he blushed a little. "What are we going to do now, Gary?"

"Well… I sorta hoped I could take you up to my place to show you my world. Would that be okay?"

"Oh, yeah! I've been waiting to see how people in New York live."

"Sure you have." He grasped Elmo's hand and walked him to his apartment building. "This is it."

Elmo tilted his head back. "Wooeee! Look at how far up it goes."

"This one is older. It has only 15 floors. Some of the big newer ones have over 50."

"Wow! That's amazing!"

"Yeah, it kind of is." And Gary started to see his own city through fresher eyes.

Once they got inside, Elmo darted over to the corner picture window. Even though Gary's building wasn't the tallest around, you could still see a few narrow vistas between some of the high rises. "This is fantastic! No wonder you like living here so much."

"Would you ever want to live here?" *Where did that come from?* "New York, I mean, not necessarily with me, you know."

"Oh, I don't know. Everybody's been so nice, and there are so many things to see and do, but I have to keep reminding myself that I have a responsibility to my family."

"As do we all…" Gary mumbled to himself. His narrow-minded parents had helped him to get established, and he still owed them a considerable amount of money. He also wondered if they'd ever grow to accept his way of life. While his job paid well, rent on this gloriously fabulous apartment took up about half his money each month.

"But I can see how people come here to New York and get all caught up in all this stuff." He looked back at Gary, "But I think I've gotten what I was supposed to get out of this adventure already."

Gary's heart staggered. Secretly, he had hopes of luring Elmo to remain in the City to fulfill his fantasies. "So… it sounds like you're ready to return to the farm."

"Hell, no!" Elmo beat the air with his fist. "You have shown me so much and been so great. I believe it's time to even up."

"Even up?"

Elmo stepped over to Gary, slowly put his arms around him and began kissing at his neck, ear, and shoulder.

"Elmo!"

"Should I stop?" His tongue licked behind Gary's ear.

"Hell, no! I just didn't think you were interested in me that way."

Two sets of lips met again, and things below began a-stirring.

Elmo pulled back and admired Gary's face. "You are the best-looking man I've ever seen. I wanted to do this–and much, much more–last night, but I had to keep in mind what my pa told me concerning matters of the heart." He squeezed Gary's hand.

"And what would that be?" Gary squeezed back.

"Never go all the way on the first date. If you're really meant to be with that person, you'll discover everything you need to know on the second date."

"Sounds like a wise man. I wish my own father had given me that piece of advice. It would have saved me so much heartache." Gary smiled at Elmo.

"No more heartache, Gary." Elmo smiled back and tapped his finger on Gary's chest, "No more heartache."

Gary tugged Elmo's hand and attempted to pull him in the direction of the bedroom. There was some resistance at first, but the two of them soon walked in tandem into Gary's inner sanctum. Fantasies began to coalesce in his mind.

"What do you like to do, Elmo?"

Elmo surveyed the room, "This is real nice. Real nice, indeed." He looked at Gary, who still had a question lingering on his face. "Oh, back where I come from, whoever has the biggest one gets to choose."

"That'll be me." Gary started to unzip his pants to free his stiffness. "I have never seen one bigger than – Oh, my! My, my, my!" Elmo had dropped his drawers and stood bottomless, pointing toward Gary. "You must have always gotten your way back home with that thing." He licked his lips and the fantasies in his head went into overdrive.

"Well, there was this one other fellow, Zeke, and he –"

"I don't want to hear about Zeke right now." Gary reached down and touched Elmo's decision winner. "What's your pleasure, Big Boy?"

Elmo grabbed Gary's hand and spun him around, front to back. Elmo began rubbing himself against Gary's smooth backside.

"Oh, Hell to the no on that! There is no way that thing is going to fit inside of me without taking out some intestines along with it." He pulled away and glowered at Elmo.

"Can you just let me show you how it's done?" Elmo reached down to his pants on the floor and retrieved a condom.

"I see you came prepared."

"We don't want to get the girls pregnant."

"Or the cows…"

"What?"

"Never mind. I was just surprised you carry your own condoms with you, that's all."

"I need a special size."

"I'm sure you do."

Once Elmo touched Gary in a sensitive way, he began to relax a bit, and when Elmo sensed that, he moved Gary to the bed and began placing his arms and legs into position.

"Take a deep breath," whispered Elmo, "and just relax. You are completely safe with me. I would never do anything to hurt you."

Gary could feel his sphincter open, wider than it had ever before. He had been afraid that it might hurt, but in this position, there was no pain at all. Within a few back-and-forth tries, Elmo was completely inside of him. It felt like sitting on the spire of the Chrysler Building.

"That's fucking amazing! Where the Hell did you learn that trick?"

"Remember that Zeke guy I was telling you about?"

"Yes, yes, but I don't want to hear any more about Zeke right now."

Elmo began thrusting slowly and gently accelerating. Gary grew concerned that his neighbors might hear the grunting and groaning flying out of the excited farm boy's throat, but then he realized he really didn't give a shit right at that moment. He began thinking about his personal fantasies, and how this fulfilled at least half of them.

The motion stopped. Elmo looked down, "Gary, why do you have your eyes closed?"

Good question. The fantasies didn't seem to be doing much good anyway. He glanced up at Elmo, who smiled down upon him, and in a flash, everything seemed to be working the way it was designed to.

He had never really tried looking at his partners during sex before. Most of the time he had retreated into his fantasies, the other person having no idea that they were merely a hunk of meat fleshing out the scenes playing in his mind.

This was different. The visual connection with Elmo was profound. He had never felt so emotional about sex before. He could feel his heart melting like dark chocolate on a sunny window sill. Here was the state of being he had been searching for, unsuccessfully, only to be led there by a visiting hick. An attractive and gentle, loving, caring man. Definitely not the type he had been encountering in Manhattan.

Elmo started grunting louder and faster, all the while locking eyes with Gary. Even Gary felt like it was almost time to let fly, but Elmo suddenly stopped and pulled out.

"What the hey?" Gary shouted. "I was just about to finish."

Elmo smiled down at him. "Not time yet. Let's switch."

So not only was the farm boy gentle, loving and caring, he was also thoughtful.

"You got one of those 'special size' bad boys for me, Elmo?"

"Let's see." He reached down into his pants pocket. "As a matter of fact, I do."

"Would you do the pleasure?"

"It would be an honor."

Within 30 seconds, Elmo had placed the condom on Gary and had him inside.

"That was easy," quipped Gary, who was used to all the complaining, whining and protesting that generally accompanied his previous attempts to fuck other guys.

"Zeke," Elmo whispered.

Gary realized he'd have to thank Zeke if he ever met him.

A few hours later, the two men had become a jumble of body parts and the bed covers hopelessly mangled. They hugged, kissed, smiled and just held each other.

"Can you stay?" Gary took the risk.

"I think so, but I should probably call the hostel and let them know. They might get concerned."

Gary didn't think there was a need to do that, but he felt it best to just let Elmo do what made him most comfortable. "Sure, we can call in a while, but let's just stay like this for now."

"Hell, yeah!" erupted Elmo.

"How long are you staying in town?" Gary's mind began mapping out a different variety of fantasy now.

Elmo lowered his eyes and looked away. "I leave for home tomorrow. I'm sorry."

Tears began to form in the creases of Gary's eyes. He realized that Elmo might not be as sophisticated and cultured as he would

have liked, but he was sincere and honest. While it might be possible to teach someone culture and sophistication, teaching honesty
and sincerity was a different matter.

What terrible karma. To meet someone with whom you
sensed a huge potential as a life partner only have them ride their
cow off into the sunrise without you on it.

"And I'm guessing they don't have phones where you live."

"Naw, but the general store does, and people call and leave
messages for us, and if we need to, we give our replies to the clerk
and they'll call back for us."

"Doesn't sound like we can leave very personal messages with
a system like that."

"No, but it's the only thing we have." Elmo looked into Gary's
dark eyes. "Unless you decide to come out and visit with me on the
farm."

Gary laughed. "That's funny. Me on a farm."

"You don't have to do chores. We have visitors all the time."

"And there'd be a place for me to stay?"

"'Course. We have a guest room in the house and a cottage on
the property."

"But what if we want to have a repeat session…?"

"There's always out behind the big barn." He laughed.

"Very funny." Gary was not laughing. "And you think they
could accept the two of us as a couple?"

"We're not overly-religious, we've made a pledge to maintain
the simple life. Besides, if I committed to taking over the dairy for

my pa, I'd imagine he'd let me shack up with a three-eyed, four-horned, purple-skinned Tasmanian Devil."

"How flattering…"

"No, you know what I mean. Times are changing, and my folks are more progressive than some of the other communities. I think once they get to know you, you would be as much a part of our family as anyone."

Once again, tears began to form in Gary's eyes. "That's very touching to hear, but, given my own folks, I have difficulty accepting it as a reality."

"Well, there's only one way to find out. Could you call the hostel for me now?"

Over the next few weeks, Elmo and Gary exchanged polite messages, fearing that all the intervening eyes might get suspicious otherwise.

One afternoon, Elmo came in from cleaning the milking stalls. His mother stopped him at the door.

"Before you bring those muddy work boots into my just-cleaned kitchen, Cousin Ruth stopped by to tell me there's a message waiting for you at the General Store." Her tone suggested suspicion, as if she wanted her son to tell her what all these confounded messages were about.

"Thanks, ma!" Elmo did an about face and trotted off to the store before his mother had a chance to ask her meddling questions.

He bounded into the General Store, careful to close the door behind him in order to keep Mr. Steinmauer from yelling at him. "You have a message for me?"

The older gentleman turned around to the counter. "Oh, it's you, Elmo. You sure have been popular lately. Who is this person from New York?" He picked up the piece of paper near the wall phone.

Elmo began to squirm. He hadn't even told his parents about his Rumspringa experience yet, and he had no desire to tell old Mr. Steinmauer, but he felt he had to say something because all roads to New York ran through him.

"Just a friend I met on Rumspringa. Thanks, Mr. Steinmauer." He snatched the note and ran outside, almost forgetting to close the door behind him.

He could hardly wait to read it. "Miss seeing you. Taking some time off. Will be there next Friday evening. Make up the guest room, and get some supplies. Gary."

Anyone strolling past who happened to look at Elmo would have witnessed the most incredible display of joy. In fact, it took a few days for his cheeks to stop stinging from all the smiling.

As best as possible, without mentioning everything, he let his parents know he was expecting a guest. His folks didn't even seem to mind. "As long as he cleans up after himself," his mother cautioned.

Friday afternoon could not arrive fast enough for Elmo. He took the family buggy to the bus station to meet his visitor. Up pulled the bus from Philadelphia, and out stepped Gary. Elmo just wanted to run up, hug and kiss him, but he realized it might not be the best thing to put on such a public display of affection. Even properly married couples wouldn't be seen doing that in public.

A plain-looking young man took Gary's bag and placed it in the back of Elmo's cart.

"Thanks, Zeke." Elmo tipped his hat.

"Zeke?" queried Gary as he tried to sneak a look at the guy's crotch.

"The very same one."

Thank you, Zeke. Gary thought to himself with a smile.

As they rode back through town, Gary noticed a gate painted the same shade of blue as the shirt he wore the evening he met Elmo. "That's the blue," he pointed.

"Yup, that it is," Elmo responded.

"What's it mean?"

The red in Elmo's face snuck up. "Umm… well… that's what parents do to let everyone else know they have a daughter in need of marrying."

"I see…" Gary mused. "So… you thought I was the farmer's daughter. Is that it?"

They both laughed, and Elmo felt relieved.

Over the next week, Elmo introduced Gary to his lifestyle. No one seemed to bother them. After each person took one look at Gary, they never made an effort to look again.

One evening after dinner, it was Gary's turn to wash the dishes, and Elmo's mother asked to see her son in the parlor.

"Elmo, I don't know exactly how to put this, but I think your father and I have figured out what's going on between you and Gary." Elmo's head dropped, but not as far as his heart had. "Don't get the wrong idea. We are not condemning you at all." Elmo looked up with hope. "We see you attempting to hide your true feeling for one another, and I think that's admirable, given the community in which we all live, but there comes a time when a man needs to take a stand and demonstrate what he's made of." She nodded.

"What are you trying to say, ma?"

She took a big breath before continuing. "We know you used your Rumspringa to explore who you really are, and you have come to accept that. Your father and I, while we, well, hoped–wished– that you would find yourself a bride, have grown to accept you and Gary as part of our family. You are our son, and nothing will ever change that."

Elmo ran over and gave his mother a big hug.

"Now, don't you be getting all New-York-City emotional over me, young man." He backed off. "Just because you spent your time off in a big city and learned yourself some new things, it does not mean you can expect your family to quickly follow along on your ride." She turned her head to one side and then looked back at Elmo. "Actually, that felt kind of good. Could you do it again, son." He gave her an even bigger hug. "Okay, that's enough. Do you think you could teach your father how to do that?" She smiled.

"Gary, are you finished?" Elmo yelled toward the kitchen.

"Just about," came the muffled reply.

"Then get yourself out here right now."

Gary raced into the parlor holding a towel. "Is everything okay?" He looked at both Elmo and his mother with concern.

Elmo stepped over to Gary, hugged him, kissed him, smiled, and said, "Everything is just fine."

They both looked over at his mother, who stood beaming with a tear drop in one eye.

The following spring, dawn broke its way into their bedroom. Elmo looked over at Gary and said, "Good morning."

"Good morning, yourself." Gary smiled.

"Ready to get up and get to work?"

"As always."

After stopping in the kitchen for their respective cups of coffee, the two men headed out across the meadow to the barn where the cows stood, waiting to be milked.

Looking for Love in All the Right Places

For some reason, the statue in Piccadilly that looks like Eros has always intrigued me. Another story in this collection uses the same location. As noted in the previous introduction, this one never made it to the editor, as the issue got cancelled before the submission deadline. Because it is narrated by an Englishman, I have used U.K. spelling.

Looking for Love in All the Right Places:

A Curator's Travel Journal

London:

The Statue of Eros in Piccadilly Circus

In the due course of my work day, I walk past Piccadilly Circus any number of times: from the Underground to my office, when I go out for my luncheon and return, lastly, when I make my way back to the Tube at the end of the day. One of the many eye-fetching sights there, a statue of Anteros, commonly referred to (rather incorrectly) as the Statue of Eros, stands atop a flattened wedding cake of tiered steps. Anteros, the brother of Eros, was the god of unrequited love, the type with which I have had the most acquaintance. Because of my line of work, I was more familiar with the actual subject of the landmark, its history and so forth, and that, perhaps, was why my love has been heretofore unrequited.

At any rate, rumour is that if you sit upon the steps beneath the sculpture, you will eventually meet the love of your life. Perhaps that's why I pass by it so often during my day, in hopes of finding my personal *Innamorata*. Or should I say *Innamorato*.

My name is Gavin, a single, gay man living in London. My profession is somewhat difficult to describe with any accuracy, but just let me call myself a curator to make it simpler. In my youth my

complexion was what others commonly referred to (rather vul-
garly) as "ginger." Now in my 30s… well, mid-30s… mid- to late-
30s, it seems more cinnamon than ginger, but there are still a few
coppery highlights that occasionally glint under bright lights. The
little horseshoes of hairline recession have just begun, and no one
but me sees them. However, I know they are there and will continue to develop until I finally look like my mother's half-bald
brother. University-educated and government-employed, I have
kept my love life sparse in order to avoid unnecessary entangle-
ments while I focused upon my career.

But as of late, like some geological time clock tick-ticking
away and pounding at my eardrums, the desire for intimate companionship has accelerated within me at a deliberate pace. Each
time I walked past that statue in Piccadilly, I browsed the questing
faces, most of them tourists anyway, hoping to make that special
connection.

This story began one late-winter morning when I needed to
dash over to Ryman to purchase more ink for the office printer. As
I passed Anteros, a set of bluish eyes followed my path and I
glanced back for a split second to get a glimpse of their owner. An
attractive young man—with short curly blond hair and a blue wool-
len jacket—sat near the top of the stairs. Definitely the type of male
form I enjoy, but he appeared to be a bit too youthful, and I told
myself I might do better to look for someone closer to my age.

On my return to the office, the blond boy's eyes followed my
progress yet again. I even allowed myself the luxury of looking at

him for more than a millisecond, and he rewarded my effort with the wisp of a smile. Oh my. He might have even fancied me. Not having time to lose at that moment, I hurried back to my office.

At midday, I walked past the statue once again, just to see if my admirer might still be there. Sure enough, parked in the same spot, the blond youth smiled as I walked past. At the Pret A Manger I grabbed for a Chicken Avocado sandwich, but I had no idea what it tasted like because all I could think about was this enticing young blond man sitting at the statue of Eros–or Anteros. I decided that if he were still there when I returned, I would screw up my courage and say hello.

As I walked back across the decorative stones all nerves, I looked to the top row for the current object of my affection. No longer there. Just as well, he looked a bit the scally. The tap on my shoulder caused me to jump like a neurotic cricket. My nerves had gotten the best of me.

"Allo, mite," came the response to my startled caper. Oh, my goodness, a Cockney, certainly from the environs of St. Mary-le-Bow. When I turned about, it was the young blond fellow, a few inches taller than I, but still a vision. I have spared you some of the auditory assault of his uneducated-sounding accent and deciphered it into more proper speech; however, I have left a few reminders here and there so you can hear it when you read. "Just wanted to say 'ello. Name's Trevor. What's yours?"

"Gavin," I managed to squeak.

"Gavin," he presented a casual, warm smile, "a pleasure." He held out his hand in a fingerless glove, which I shook like a robot. "Noticed ya cupla times today. Fit. Right fit, y'are."

"Ummm, thank you, Tr-Trevor." I pulled my hand back and tightened my coat while my brain skidded across two lanes of on-coming traffic. I think I blurted out, "Nice to meet you, but I've got to get back to my office now."

"Yeh, right. See ya 'round." He wiggled his fingers as I ran off like a pathetic coward.

Prague:

The National Gallery, Veletržní Palace

The next week my work had me going on a tour about the Continent conducting research for a new project. Prague was the initial stop, and my first free evening I decided to play tourist and take in the National Gallery. While modern art was not my fa-vourite, I wanted to give their collection a look-see. As the building was labelled a "palace," I had hoped it would look like one of the many historic building with turrets, dormers, and glorious Gothic elements scattered throughout the old city. Unfortunately, it had a blocky, modernist look to it, nothing remarkable to mention.

My attention focused on a painting depicting a mostly-naked man clinging to some level crags above a cloudy beach. A leopard skin draped between his legs covered his groin. The look of an-guish upon his face demonstrated the artist's ability to capture the human spirit when not at its best, a look I have felt many times in desperation.

"Gavin! Whatcha doin' 'ere?"

What are the odds? The young Trevor appeared like magic in a modern art gallery hundreds of miles away from home.

"Trevor, isn't it?" I inquired in a monotone, and he nodded. I did not wish to appear overly eager to see him again. So soon. "Shouldn't it be me asking you that question?"

"Fair 'nuff," came his terse reply. "Me gran's on a bit of a go-round, an' she wanted me with 'er." His charming smile outweighed his lack of charming speech. "An' you?"

"Well"–how to explain–"I'm here on a sort of busman's holiday."

"Ohhhhh… You a busman?"

"No," I chuckled, "I'm what you might call a curator, and I'm looking to –"

"Like a perfesser?" he interrupted, pointing a slightly dirty finger at me.

I coughed. "Yes, something like that. Yeah…"

He indicated the painting, "I sees ya fancies the Fox."

Fox? The only living thing in the painting was the distraught, nearly-naked man.

"Yeah, the artist's name is Liška, an' 'at means 'fox' in Czech."

Very impressive. "Do you speak Czech, Trevor?"

"Naw, naw. I just read it there." He pointed to the interpretive card. "Now me," he pointed at himself, "I prefers Zrzavý. There's your painter."

"I must confess, I've never heard of him. Are any of his works here?"

"Naw, naw. They've all been sold at auction, they 'ave. 'E's painted a few nude boys." Trevor shrugged and winked at me. "But there's one of 'em what looks a bit like me, and now that I think of it, there's one that favours you, too."

I think this might have been a compliment, at least that was how I chose to interpret it. Otherwise, Bob's not my uncle.

"'Course their bits is a bit small, if ya ketch me drift." He laughed, and obnoxious electronic music began to play from his coat pocket. Trevor reached inside and pulled out a mobile. After looking at the display, he announced, "It's me gran. Gotta run. Cheers!"

So utterly charming, that one. A real prince. But at least he knew something about modern Czech art. I'd have to look up that Zrzavý he mentioned.

Florence:

Galleria dell'Accademia, Michelangelo's Statue of David

Florence was the next stop, and I strolled from my hotel across the Arno upon the Ponte Vecchio–with its collection of "love locks" left by ardent Florentine lovers–to spend some time at the

Uffizi. Realizing the original statue of David was not too far away, I decided to take a gander.

When asked how he was able to produce such fine works of sculpture, Michelangelo supposedly responded: "Every block of stone has a statue inside it, and it is the task of the sculptor to discover it." Of course, he spoke Italian, and it may have lost something in translation. That said, I have no idea how he discovered such immense beauty within a chunky lump of limestone before starting this spectacular masterpiece.

"Quite life-like innit, eh perfesser?" Trevor? Yet again? "'Course these bits is more life-size." He giggled.

I turned to him, "Trevor, I'm sorry, but–I must say–it appears as if you are following me."

"Oh, naw, perfesser. Jes' a coincidence." He nodded. "Seems like you 'n me likes the same arts." He smiled.

"Yes, so it seems."

"Now, the eyes aren't quite right, but I'm willin' t'givvim the benefits of the doubt 'ere." That was true. Of all the details, the eyes were the least accurate. "An' 'e could do with a bit of a 'aircut, mindya."

Now I laughed. "Trevor, I find your interpretation most amusing." I continued to study the sculpture.

"Thank ya, perfesser. Thank ya."

"Oh, I'm not a professor"–I turned to him–"just a curator."

"Whatever." He tossed his hand. "But what a beautiful 'n fit man 'e is." He tilted his head to David.

"Not exactly my type." My head turned to Trevor.

"Well then, what exactly might be your type?" he queried.

I had to stall a breath to keep from spitting out the honest truth. Then I remembered what my idle curiosity had found for me. "I did look up your Czech artist…"

"Zrzavý?"

"Yes, that's the one. What an interesting style he had."

"Quite right, mite." He smiled with boyish impertinence.

"The painting you referred to that you felt looked like you, well, I see the resemblance is quite remarkable, except for the hair being trimmed so close."

"Yeh, that's me all right, 'septin' the bits. Mine are more life-size, they are." He smiled again and waggled his eyebrows.

"Of course." And wouldn't I have wanted to see them. Not the time nor the place. "And the one you thought looked like me…"

"*The Sleepin' Boy?*"

"Yes. I can see somewhat of a parallel, but I haven't looked like that in, oh, many a year."

"An' I'm sure the bits is much bigger, too!" His eyebrows raised.

I could feel my flushed face reddening even further. "Well, I wouldn't say…" and our eyes locked for the first time. My heart stopped, my breath stopped, my brain stopped.

"Like what ya see, mite?"

When my body began to function again, I coughed into my fist, a feeble attempt to cover my embarrassment. "Well, you certainly are a good-looking lad."

"Yeh, well I kinda likes the way ya looks, too, I do." One side of his mouth curled up a little, *á la* Mona Lisa, and his eyes shifted into bedroom mode.

"Thanks," I squeaked.

Seconds of uncomfortable silence ensued while I tried to look at anything but him or David. My mind kept telling me I'm too old for him, but another part of my body announced he was more attractive than the statue next to us. And Trevor was a live one.

"Um, still traveling with your grandmother?" was the only thing I could think of that did not have anything whatsoever to do with bit sizes or mutual attraction.

"Oh, yeh. She's about 'ere somewhere..." He looked round.

"Well, I must meet her, then. Let's go look for her," I suggested. Perhaps meeting his grandmother might explain a few things.

For the first time since we began encountering each other, he balked and blushed. "Errrr, that might not be such a good idea..."

Hmmmm... that sparked my curiosity. "All right. I trust she is well."

"All well, all well she is, yeh."

This time my mobile rang. Project supervisor calling. "Sorry, Trevor, my turn to run off. Job. Boss. You know..."

"Right. See ya round."

Warsaw:
Saski Park Fountain

I felt the splash of water on my face as I approached the gorgeous old, circular fountain in the centre of Saski Park (site of former Polish palaces and one of the oldest public spaces in Continental Europe). This helped to wash away hours of laborious research I had just completed. Much like the statue in Piccadilly Circus, this fountain served as a place for the amorous to meet, and several young couples strolled the maze of manicured pathways.

Closing my eyes felt refreshing as well, but when I opened them again, I could see Trevor through the falling droplets, across the plaza, staring into the sprays above the large bowl. My first thought was to turn and walk away before anything further could develop. It had been like a silly schoolboy thing at first, but we kept running into each other in rather surprizing foreign places. From his behaviour at Florence, it seemed fairly certain he had an interest in me, but I wasn't so sure I still maintained a similar interest in him.

Mind you, I was not ashamed of my orientation, and I would not alter it—even if I could—but discussing sexual matters in public was a bit much. My conservative upbringing did not allow for such things. Too crude and vulgar for me.

Yes, I should have done a turnabout and left as quickly as possible. Yes, that was exactly what I should have done. However, I stood unmoving. Watching him watch the fountain captivated me. With all his abrasive edges, he still managed to have a peculiar and cultivated appreciation of art. At least he did not use that annoying and indecipherable Cockney rhyming slang.

Trevor raised his arm and started waving to me. I had been caught and could not run. What in blazes was I so afraid of?

"What a coincidence! Fancy meetin' up with you again. Howya been?"

At least he did not start off discussing the size of our male organs. Perhaps I should–at minimum–give him another chance to demonstrate his good intentions.

"Just admiring the fountain. You?"

"Yeh, yeh, the same." He gave me the once over. "Say, if ya really, really likes fountains, there's an amazin' sounds 'n lights show this *h*evenin' over at Square One." Trevor pointed in the direction of the Wisła River.

Well, it would give us some time to get to know each other a little better. And I didn't really have any place to be at that moment. So, why the heck not?

"Sure, let's go, but if you don't mind, could we stop somewhere along to the way to get a bite. I'm famished." After all, it was my first time in Warsaw, and he seemed to have a better working knowledge of this area than I.

"I know jes' the place. Folla me!" And off he started. I paused for an instant to take in his rear view. Quite nice, actually.

A few blocks away, in Weirzbowa street, we came to Patrick's Irish Pub. Not the kind of thing one would expect to find in the capital of Poland.

"A bit of 'ome, innit." He pointed at the pub with his stubby thumb. "Ya fancy?"

I had been away for a while and missed some of my favs. Perhaps they served a Bubble and Squeak that would remind me of my own local haunt. "Sure."

The Polish version of British cuisine fared adequate at best, as was to be expected. We chatted quite a bit about art we both liked. I had, after all, uncovered some charm within him; it just needed to be coaxed out.

From there we walked to the riverfront and followed a walkway to the Multimedia Park Fountain. While not my cup of tea–as one might say–the loud music and stroboscopic lights proved to be a nice distraction, even if a bit too modern for my Old-World tastes.

After about thirty minutes of observing the show–and Trevor–both our mobiles rang simultaneously. We laughed and answered in synchrony. After spouting brief "Cheers!" we went off to our respective destinations.

St. Petersburg:

The Hermitage, Fine Art Collection

I stood in front of a painting by Fragonard entitled *The Stolen Kiss*. It portrayed a late 18th-Century woman leaning towards a door, through which a figure (not certain whether it was male or female) leaned in and kissed her on the cheek.

My concentration broke when my own cheek received a stolen kiss.

"Jes' like them in the paintin'," joked Trevor. He sure had some cheek himself.

My head swivelled left then right, looking to see if anyone saw us. "Trevor! That kind of behaviour can get us arrested here. They don't look kindly on same-sex couples in Russia."

His eyebrows jumped up. "Ya sayin' we's a couple now, are ya?" He started to move in for a hug.

When I drew back, Trevor appeared surprised. "I am here on *business*, and if I get detained for any reason, I could be made redundant."

"Oh, sorry, perfesser." His eyes dropped, and he appeared contrite, a side of him he had not previously displayed. "It's jes' I've taken a right likin' to ya, y'know. Thassall."

"It's okay, Trevor. There's no one around, but if they review the closed-circuit, we might be in for a bit of questioning. Perhaps we should move about."

Over the next hour or so we gazed up and around at the amazing collection of art, which included works of Botticelli, Gainsborough, Rembrandt, Watteau, Renoir, Monet, Van Gogh, Gauguin, Cézanne, Degas, Matisse, Picasso, and so many others. It was the longest we had ever spent looking at art together. He continued to display his wide-reaching comprehension of fine art while he worked his boyish charm upon me. It was a pity that we were in a country where taking things to the next level might be considered a crime.

As I learned more about Trevor, it became clear that his manner of speech hid his true nature nearly the whole nine yards. At times he was full of beans and expressed himself like a Royal Marine on shore leave, but when we discussed art, he presented himself as a well-educated expert.

When closing time arrived, we each went our separate ways. And for some niggling reason, I had a sense I would continue to see more of him.

Barcelona:
Basílica de la Sagrada Família, Nativity Façade

Seeing the sculpted image of a tortoise squashed beneath a column near the entrance made me chuckle to myself. I saw it as a representation of my non-existent love life: never moving, but even if it could have, progress would have been quite slow at that.

I had been in Barcelona for two days with no sign of Trevor. Could he have been put off by our last encounter in Russia? That would have been difficult for me to accept because he had seemed more interested than ever. Was I actually looking forward to seeing him again? What has happened to me? I should have been thanking my lucky stars he ceased tracking me across the Continent.

"Sorry I'm late, perfesser." Just at that moment Trevor ran up, panting. "Our train got delayed in Zagreb with engineerin'."

"What a pleasant surprise, Trevor. I can't say I'm shocked to see you." He smiled and my heart went all alight.

"Nice. Nice to know." He reached out to hug me, and this time I did not stop him. His heavy breathing went on for about half a minute. My nose perceived his musky aroma, and I smiled.

People–presumably other tourists–passed by, pointing, but not at us. I followed their fingers and saw the object of their interest–of course–the church.

"Trevor," I uttered when we eased up on the hug, "I am growing curious as to why you keep showing up wherever I happen to be."

"Yeh, well," he hesitated, "I can't rightly explain it all to ya right now-like, but please–please–believe me what all will be cleared up soon. I promise ya," and he held up a few fingers like a Battersea Boy Scout. "All ya needs to know izzat, well…, izzat, well"–he got really cute when tongue-tied–"I'm 'opin' this can lead to somethin' really, really great."

I could not help but revel at his discomfiture. The forthrightness melted my resolve and heightened my curiosity as to whether anything could develop between the two of us, dissimilar as we seemed. However, there were a few concerns I needed to address.

"Trevor, one of the things I have apprehensions about is the difference in our ages. I'm in my 30s, well, mid-30s, and –"

"Blimey!" It's been a long while since I've heard anyone utter that old chestnut. "An' 'ere I was, worried that I might be too ol' for ya." He laughed aloud, disarming me.

"You think I'm only interested in young boys?"

"No, perfesser. I'm likely older than ya might think." And when I looked closer, I could see slight wrinkles around his eyes I had not noticed before. Perhaps we were closer in age than I had previously believed. "I took a few gap years abroad afore 'ittin' the uni. Wanted to make a go of it first. When things didn't work out the way I 'ad 'oped, I went 'ome, an' me folks sent me off to Oxford."

Oxford? He hadn't struck me as the Oxford type. I only went to the University of East London. I hoped he wouldn't hold that against me.

"So… you like architecture?" I asked, pointing at the work of art we stood next to.

"It's all right. It's all right, I s'pose. Kinda like giant sculptures, they is."

Giant sculptures. I s'pose one can see it that way, especially in the work of Gaudí. His building designs gave the impression of liveable art more than merely functional buildings. It's a shame he died so young. Mind the street cars, I say.

I suggested getting a meal together, and we walked to the Café Gaudí in Carrer de Sardenya nearby. Over a tapas snack, we discussed getting together once we returned to London to see if things might just work out between the two of us. Once I learned we were closer in age than I had imagined—and that his education surpassed mine—my last few inhibitions fell away. I found him attractive, and he seemed interested in me for some reason I could not fathom. However, figuring out *that* particular part was not of particular import to me in the moment.

I had a ticket for the late afternoon express train, and we were not able to spend more than an hour together. I made sure I gave him my contact information so that we could connect back home.

For once, the thought of seeing him again did not wrack my nerves.

Paris:
Pont de l'Archevêché

Following completion of my final duties before returning home, I decided to walk about the picturesque streets of Paris. Feeling a bit of the romantic, I let my curiosity get the best of me, and I strolled from Île de la Cité across the Pont de l'Archevêché to see the local display of love locks.

Over the years, Parisian lovers have placed padlocks along metal railings the length of Pont des Arts and Pont de l'Archevêché. To signify their commitment to one another and symbolize their eternal romance, the couple would toss the key into the river Seine below, similar to what had been done on the Ponte Vecchio in Florence.

Knowing that Trevor and his grandmother have been trailing me this whole time, I did not expect that it would take long for him to appear out of nowhere. As if on cue, the lovely young fellow came walking towards me from the other side of the bridge. My chest went light and giddy. This time, a mature woman, more like a dowager, accompanied him. The mysterious Gran!

As they came closer, I realized I recognized this woman! She held a position on the board of directors of my agency. Not a direct supervisor, but definitely someone who knew of my work, and most certainly someone who knew about my exploratory excursions.

"Gavin! Heya!" shouted Trevor as they approached. I nodded, specifically to his grandmother. "I believe ya know me Gran."

She grinned with tight lips. "Gavin, how nice to see you."

"And nice to see you, mum. A bit unexpected, but rather pleasant, nonetheless."

"Yes, I expect you had no idea as to why my grandson has been dogging you about the Continent." She smiled with reserve. I could only imagine her daughter must have strayed into Cheapside for her to have a grandchild the likes of Trevor.

"No, mum. It has been a bit of a mystery, you could very well say." I studied her face for clues, but her muscles had tightened up so many years ago they seemed to no longer respond to her veiled emotions.

"Well, I shall now explain everything to you, Gavin, as I believe you do deserve an explanation." She pointed to the railing with locks on it. "Shall we step out of the way of foot traffic?"

The three of us moved towards the large metallic display of public affection. It truly amazed me how many locks filled the grate. Paris was, without doubt, the city of love. I couldn't have imagined anything like this ever happening in London.

Trevor smickered at me and remained uncharacteristically quiet. Perhaps the proximity of his grandmother caused his vocal cords to malfunction the same way mine did in her presence at the office.

"My grandson here," she grasped Trevor's arm, "is very... special to me, and needs someone in his life to guide him forward and care for him. Someone of solid character and fortitude." She looked at me. "I believe he requires what you might call a *curator*." A sly smile spread her mouth. "I hope you don't mind that I arranged these chance meetings in order to provide you an opportunity to get to know him a bit better."

I swung my head in Trevor's direction with a surprised scowl on my face. His chin sunk to his chest.

"Now, I know this is uncommon–very uncommon indeed–but I needed to know if the two of you would be... well... appropriate for each other."

Trevor looked up at me with a mischievous grin.

"My grandson has spoken quite highly of you, and I am well acquainted with your work, Gavin. You have earned my respect, and that is not something I can say to very many people at all."

I looked back at Trevor with a similar mischievous grin.

"From everything he has told me, it appears that you two have... rather taken a liking to each other." She looked at me, then at her grandson. "I trust you find him suitable." The decorous older woman displayed her own mischievous grin.

Trevor's moist eyes asked a question that his lips could not. My own eyes started to tear up, and my brows began to knit. "M-M-Most suitable, mum." My mouth formed an unexpected grin as I glanced at the unexpected object of my unexpected affection.

The sound of brass jingling cut the air. His grandmother held out an old-fashioned hotel key, the kind with a metal room number tag.

As she handed it to Trevor, she admonished, "Now, gentlemen, I shall be walking over to Notre Dame to take the afternoon tour with a docent. I expect I shall make it back to the hotel round about—say—half past six o'clock, and we shall all dine together. Please be cleaned up and ready to go by the time I return." She winked at me and tottered away, treading at a turtle's pace towards Île de la Cité.

London:

The Statue of Eros in Piccadilly Circus

Rumour is that if you sit upon the steps beneath the Statue of Eros—or Anteros, more accurately—you will eventually meet the love of your life. On a recent, hunky-dory afternoon, I sat perched atop the pedestal watching people pass to and fro, mostly tourists. Some looked at each other for the very first time, others for the very last.

Billions of us share this mammoth, miraculous marble as it floats through the inky heavens, but every so often—once in a double blue moon or so—just being in the right place at the right time makes all the difference in the world.

A voice rang out and caught my ear. "Oy! Perfesser!"

The sound of Trevor's voice brought an impish smile to my face. He stepped up through the crowd, hugged and kissed me. "Oy, yerself!" I replied.

"Are ya ready to eat?" Trevor inquired while delving into my shy green eyes with his wild cornflower ones.

He extended a hand and clasped mine to assist me with standing. We descended the stairs to the street together. "How does Pret A Manger sound?"

Stag Station

Prompts for writing sometimes come from the oddest of places (and that's what makes them so interesting!). I had heard a news article about a lighthouse off the coast of San Francisco, and this story came out of my twisted imagination. I submitted it to the Saints + Sinners collection for 2020, but it did not make the cut.

Stag Station

"What exactly is a stag station?" I asked the recruiter.

"No women, no families," came the gruff reply. "You married?" he pointed a stubby, furrowed finger toward me.

"No, sir." I would have liked to have been married, but a man can't marry another man. The recent ending of my clandestine relationship had spurred me toward looking into this job as a lighthouse keeper's assistant. "It's just me."

A glassy eye gave me a fleeting inspection. "Yeah, you'll be fine," he muttered, then coughed deeply and resonantly. It sounded like he had smoked many cigarettes for many years. "How soon can you start?" he asked as he continued to scribble on some form with the stump of a well-chewed pencil.

"I'm ready immediately, sir."

"That's good. We need someone immediately." His smile unnerved me as he hadn't shaved in a few days and he had several missing teeth. "We can't leave Platon alone for very long."

"Platon?" I echoed.

"The lighthouse keeper. Good guy, but a little strange." The recruiter waivered a flattened hand in the air near his head as he scratched behind the other ear with the little bit of pencil. "Most guys don't last more than a month with him, but I got a special feelin' 'bout you." Again, he pointed at me.

I had a special feeling about the man I recently tore myself away from. Two years of sneaking around to spend time with him tore my soul open a bit too often. The note I left behind explained exactly how I felt.

After a hard swallow, I said, "I would like to believe that I can get along with just about anybody."

A loud laugh reverberated around the cramped office walls swathed in old calendars and nautical charts, exposing more of the man's gums with missing teeth. "Yeah. Let's wait a few days before makin' any more of them judgments, you hear." He handed me a piece of paper and pointed out the door. "Take this here form to the harbormaster over there."

I stood, took the paper, hoisted my kit bag over a shoulder. "Thank you, sir."

The smile reappeared on the grizzled face. "Don't be thankin' me just yet, fella."

The inside of the cavernous customshouse reverberated with conversation and mechanical noises. I stepped into the harbormaster's office and presented the form.

Within an hour the small motor boat propelled a pilot, my bag and me out through the Golden Gate, passing the old Civil War fort standing guard. The cold water sprayed up on my face, tasting bitter and salty, like tears. Mist occluded the view, and I could not tell where we traveled. Every so often, a loud, low-pitched belch, like the roar of God, resonated my head. About ten minutes later, the engine slowed, and the boat approached a tiny rock in the middle of nowhere.

We pulled up to a small metal platform, and the pilot pointed wordlessly to it. Even if he had said anything, I wouldn't have been able to hear it over the crashing of the waves. I tossed my bag onto the landing and then grabbed the wet, rusty metal, pulling myself onto the miniscule island that looked more like a submarine conning tower.

When I tilted my head back, I could barely make out the shape of the lighthouse. It appeared to be tiered, like a wedding cake, rather than the tapered, traditional smooth shape. When I considered the job as a lighthouse keeper's assistant, I figured I'd be placed somewhere remote, but at least on land. This isolated, diminutive island would never have entered my imagination.

A rickety, curved stairway wound about the rock, and I slowly made my way up. Frequently I would have to pause as menacing waves lapped at the base, and I preferred not to be a casualty on my first day at the job. Again, the deafening belching noise repeated at steady intervals, even louder now that I had arrived at its source.

When I reached the platform, I saw a gray, metal door and rapped upon it. After a few seconds of waiting, I knocked again, a bit harder. It finally occurred to me that the loud noises of the sea drowned out any sounds I might be making, and I pushed the cold, iron handle down. The door opened easily, and I stepped into what I can only describe as a mechanical engine room. Compressors and oil-fueled generators whirred noisily. There was barely enough light coming through the smoke-stained windows to make out a stairway, which I climbed up.

The next level appeared more like a small apartment with a desk, books piled high on one side, a sink and sideboard across the way, and a rickety table with two spindly chairs against the curved wall.

"Hello?" I called out.

"Who the hell is there?" croaked a gruff voice from above. Footsteps on the ceiling traversed to the top of the stairs, and a shadow appeared. The person descending would be difficult to classify. Neither young nor old, not handsome or plain, neither dark nor light, not tall or short. His face had creased into a permanent scowl, and his dark-brown hair framed it in an unruly outline. He wore a gray uniform stained with dark splotches.

"Are you Platon?" I squeaked.

"Who the hell are you?" he growled.

I explained how the recruiter selected me to be the keeper's assistant. He grunted intermittently.

"Hmmmpf!" With one of his muscular arms, he motioned me to the stairs. "Come on up, Greenie."

"Greenie? But my name is –"

"Doesn't matter what your name is, you're Greenie now." He disappeared up the stairs and I followed.

Second and third thoughts began to swirl about in my head. I wanted to be away from the rest of humanity, but I wasn't sure this was the human I wanted to be trapped in a sardine can with. Then again, getting my mind off my troubles might be just what I needed.

I could see why they did not want women here. A small, cramped place surrounded by sea swells. This could have never provided the comforts of a home.

When we reached the next floor, I saw three cots and a latrine. One of the cots had disheveled sheets. A small stairway led further up.

"Choose your bunk," Platon barked.

"Will there be three of us?" I inquired.

He made a clicking noise with his cheek that sounded extremely dismissive. "Nah. The other one is only for emergency visitors."

I dropped my bag on the cot furthest from the unkempt one, figuring he didn't want to be close to me either. Without warning or asking, he stepped to the primitive toilet, undid his trousers and began peeing. I wanted to look–I didn't want to look. The sound of the splashing water rankled my ears.

When he stepped away from the toilet, I waited to see if he went to the sink to wash his hands, but he did not. Instead, he went to the stairs and began to climb. Midway up, he turned and motioned me to follow.

The next level up contained storage and look-out stations. A metal ladder led up to the light mechanism. Platon stood on the only space available, and I positioned myself on the ladder so that my head poked up above the flooring. With so much machinery crammed into the glass enclosure, only one person could occupy it at a time.

A giant Fresnel lens in a shiny brass frame occupied most of the room. The huge gears for turning the lens seemed imposing and dangerous. In the midst of the great, glass heart of the lighthouse sat the oil-vapor lamp, larger than anything I had ever seen before.

Through the window plates I could barely make out the shoreline of San Francisco across the water. If I wanted to get away from everyone, this seemed like the ideal place. No one could just walk up to the front door and knock.

Platon showed me the controls for the great lamp and explained how the mechanism worked. We were to ignite it one half-hour before sunset and extinguish it one half-hour after sunrise.

There would be much to do in maintaining the lighthouse. Daily inspections of equipment, weather reporting, cleaning and polishing the lens and its housing. The smoke left by the oil-vapor lamp permeated just about everything in the lighthouse.

"This job of lighthouse keeper seems monumental," I said casually, making an attempt at human conversation as we descended to the level with the cots.

"I ain't no keeper, Greenie," he squawked. "I'm a tender."

That seemed a rather odd statement as I sensed nothing tender about him.

The building abruptly shook, and I reached my hand to a nearby wall to steady myself. "Was that an earthquake?" I pondered out loud.

"Nah," he retorted. "Sometimes the waves hit the sides pretty hard. You'll get used to it."

He stripped out of his uniform and began washing himself at the basin. Again, I wanted to look, but I didn't want to look. Curiosity got the better of me, and when I caught a glimpse of his manhood, I shuddered a bit. The action of cleaning must have inadvertently aroused him, and I might have stared a bit longer than I should have. His distended member formed a gently curving arc that pointed downward. I had never seen one shaped such as this before! It enticed me, and I began thinking about the possibilities for something so magnificent and different.

"You hungry?" he asked, breaking me free from my momentary fantasy.

Yes, I was hungry, but perhaps not in the manner he had intended.

We walked down a level, and he opened the cupboard filled with tins. Columns and columns of preserved food stood awaiting disposition. His hand snatched a can of beans and the opening device. I watched in awe as he made quick work of the top, piercing and rotating, piercing and rotating, over and over until the metal flap rose majestically and magically.

I stepped closer and peered inside the cabinet. Salmon, sardines, beans, beans, and more beans. Several columns had accumulated layers of smoke and could not be easily read. I grabbed one of the grimy cans and began to wipe the film to reveal Mixed Vegetables.

"I don't eat those," he mumbled as he pointed with a beat-up spoon at the can in my hand. "You can have 'em all, far as I'm concerned." He went back to shoveling tepid beans into his maw.

My attempts at opening a can seemed to amuse him. I had never worked such a device before, and the little blade kept folding back onto the shaft before I could get very far. Finally, he set his can down with the old spoon sticking up out of it, walked over and took the can and the opener from me.

"Like this," he demonstrated as I observed. About halfway around, he grabbed my hand and placed it on the opening device, wrapped his hand around mine and began operating it. Once we had reached the point where the lid rose, he put down the opener and handed me a rather clean-looking spoon. "See. It ain't that hard."

Actually, something of mine had gotten hard during this training session. Without thinking about it, nor wanting it, my own manhood had become aroused. Was it his touch? his smell? the unanticipated intimacy?

The spoon fell from my hand and I bent to retrieve it. Platon let a quiet laugh escape his crusty lips. "You have a lot to learn, Greenie!"

I couldn't be certain, but it did seem as though he took a gander at my backside when I stooped down. Apparently, I did have much to learn.

After noisily munching through the contents of his can, Platon opened the window above the sink and tossed the empty container out into the boisterous spray. Before I opened my mouth to chastise him for such appalling behavior, my logical mind suggested it might be due to the lack of space in the lighthouse. I could only imagine how quickly garbage might pile up if we did not have adequate room for it.

As I nibbled on the slimy, lukewarm chunks of vegetables, Platon kept glancing at me from time to time. His peculiar manners continued to rattle my nerves, and his not-very-surreptitious scrutiny agitated my already-uneasy stomach.

Having reached the bottom of the tin, I placed the spoon in the sink, opened the window and reluctantly tossed the can out. For a brief moment, I felt oddly giddy, manly, suddenly empowered by my sea-fouling action. I might have even smiled.

He ascended the stairs and waved me along. At the next level Platon ordered, "Put those on," pointing at a neatly-folded uniform placed atop my cot.

I had never gotten accustomed to others looking at my unrobed body, and having to change clothing in front of this lummox stirred up all the anxiety and dread I had ever experienced. Knowing we would be spending almost all of our time together for quite a while, my logical mind realized he might be seeing me in my undergarments rather frequently. A loud, staccato blast echoed, and a foul odor followed a second later. Such animal behavior!

I mustered up all the resolve I could. Facing away from him, I fumbled with buttons and clasps, removing my own shirt and pants. As I donned the slightly-wrinkled uniform, I could sense his eyes moving up and down the side of my body facing him.

"Let's go," he called when I had finished changing. "I want to show you the rest of the place."

He started down the stairs and I followed. On the level with the desk, he showed me the paperwork I would be dealing with. I assumed that he probably did not know how to read or write, and that left the record-keeping work to the assistant. On the wall hung a weather station, with readings for temperature, wind direction and speed, humidity, and barometric pressure. Each day I was to report the conditions on a log.

One shelf held manuals and I had realized I had not brought any books with me. "Is there anything else to read around here other than those?" I pointed to the manuals.

Platon stepped to the table and picked up what looked like a well-thumbed Bible. "This is the only book I ever need." He dropped it with a thud. "Come on." He started down the stairs to the mechanical level.

He explained what each of the machines did. One supplied electricity for the gear mechanism, another compressed air for the horn. The extremely loud horn that wore away at my eardrums every time it blasted forth its hellish air blast. Thankfully, we only started that up when visibility conditions diminished significantly.

Next to one of the behemoth contraptions I spied a wooden trapdoor. "What's down there?" I asked nonchalantly.

"Don't ever go down there!" he shouted back, as if protecting me from some inconceivable horror. "That's just the tanks. Fuel oil and our fresh water." One of his eyes squinted slightly. "There's no need to go below this deck."

"Okay," I responded with a nervous laugh.

"Once a month, the boys from Goat Island come out and top us off." He smiled. "Sometimes it can be a real… social event …" Platon started up the stairs. "Let's go!" he ordered, and I followed.

From the cupboard he retrieved two brown bottles. At the table, he placed one of them at the edge and pulled down, sending the crown cap flying across the room. As he handed me the bottle, he said, "I hope you like beer."

Beer? I had never tasted alcohol in my life! Beer? Where did it come from, and how much trouble would we be in if anyone found us with it?

"The water ain't that good for drinking, and this stuff"–he popped the cap off the other bottle and took a swig–"is all we have." A loud belch erupted from his gullet.

Holding the bottle in my trembling hand, I read the inscription–"Golden Gate Bottling Works"–running in an arch on one side and found an embossed image of a bear on the other. I lifted it and inhaled lightly. A few earthy bubbles tickled my nose, and I giggled involuntarily.

Platon observed my activity in relative silence as he continued to suck the suds from his own bottle.

Who brought this? When? How did you get it? My mind reeled off unnecessary questions. "Are we going to get in trouble for having this?"

"Just drink it."

I positioned the opening to my cold lips and tilted back. The first splash tasted like prison. A bitter, toxic-tasting brew assaulted my mouth. If I had been alone, I would have spit it out immediately. My face screwed up into a contorted display of disgust as I attempted to swallow.

"You'll get used to it," came the advice from across the way.

Somehow, I sensed that would not be the last time he would use that phrase.

After he had pulled the bottle dry, he went to the window and tossed it out. Back home, I never threw glass bottles away because we could get a return deposit for them. However, out here, I imagined there might not be a place that collected illegal beer bottles.

Platon picked the old book off the table and headed up the stairs. I began to follow, and he held his hand out. "I'm going to be up there a while. Just wait for me here."

I perused the volumes on the shelf. Maintenance manuals, instruction booklets, regulations. Every so often I heard what sounded like stomping and a few grunts from above. What kind of person made those types of noises while reading a Bible?

Drinking alcohol had been illegal most of my life, and there I stood with a bottle of beer in my hand. It kind of made sense that if you were going to violate the law, this little rock in the middle of nowhere might be a good place to avoid arrest. Another attempt at sipping the bitter swill did not improve the taste, but if I wanted to avoid catching dysentery, typhoid, or cholera, I had better get used to it, as Platon had advised.

To take my mind off the situation, I gazed out the window to the west and watched the sun slowly set. Before long, the burning ball approached the waves on the horizon.

"Come on up," came the cry from above. "It's time to perform our duty."

I set the nasty bottle down and climbed up the stairs. When I reached the level with the great lamp, Platon stood on the only spot for a person. He tugged a chain from his pocket. A watch followed, and he gave it a good look, as if attempting to foretell the future.

With no action from the tender himself, hissing gas ignited, the light burst into intense brightness, nearly blinding me, and the giant lens began to rotate on its own. I raised an arm to shield my eyes.

"How did it do that?" I asked, agog. "Aren't we supposed to push some buttons or something?"

Platon grinned and let a small laugh escape his crooked mouth. "It's aut-o-matic." He pointed to a brass tube sitting above the light housing. "That there's the sun valve. It knows when the sun sets and rises. Fancy little thing."

"Then why are we even here?" seemed like a logical question.

"What if it don't work? Somebody's got to turn the light on, Greenie."

The lighthouse could function without human intervention, yet there we were. Guardians of the essential flame.

As he descended the scrawny ladder, Platon pushed me out of the way without a word. I followed him to the pantry and watched him pull another can of beans from the shelf.

"Help yourself," he mumbled.

I found a can with no label and decided to take a gamble. I fumbled with the flimsy opening device but kept at it until the lid began to rise on its own. Inside I found little sausages. They probably would have tasted better warm, but we had no stove, and I merely pulled them one-at-a-time from the can with my unblemished fingers.

While I dined, I watched the sun set below the Pacific Ocean, gently lighting it from beyond the horizon before extinguishing to near darkness. The beacon above circled monotonously, and I soon became mesmerized by its rhythm.

After gritting my teeth and disposing of the can through the window, I went to the cot where I had placed my bag earlier. The events of the day had exhausted me, and I lay down just for a moment. With nary a stray thought, I fell into a deep slumber.

I woke to ringing bells and horn blasts. Through the window I could see a small ship sitting next to our little island home.

"Hello, gorgeous!" said a voice I did not recognize from a face I had never seen before. And what a face! Rosy and fine with brilliant blue eyes. Eyes that lowered to my midsection, where an unexpected protrusion had remained from a latent dream, I imagined.

He wiggled his eyebrows at me. "If only I had time to help you with that, pal." A swirling whistle escaped his plump lips. "Perhaps next time we call you can help me in the pump room." The eyebrows danced once more. "My name is Chip," he announced as he approached, arm outstretched.

With little thought, I covered my embarrassment with my left hand and took his right in mine. "It's a pleasure to meet you, Chip. My name is – "

"Greenie!" he chirped. "Platon told us. Welcome aboard!" When he smiled, one side of his lips raised a bit higher than the other. "We're your support crew from Goat Island. We brought you some fresh supplies. Is there anything you might be wanting?" His stare suggested the question might be somewhat open-ended.

At that moment, I realized I had more than one immediate desire. "Yes, Chip," I managed to squeak. "Would it be possible for you to bring us some soda?"

He giggled. "We already bring you all the soda"–he winked in an obvious manner–"from the *soda shop*"–he winked twice–"we can."

"No," it took me a second to realize he had been referring to the beer as 'soda.' "I mean real soda–pop–whatever you might call it. Nehi, something like that."

"Ohhhh, soda," he mimicked musically. "Sure. Sure. Next time we'll bring you some *soda*." He winked again. "Come on," he waved me toward the stairs. "You might want to give Platon a hand with the supplies.

I followed Chip down to the mechanical room. A door stood open, and through it I could see some kind of metal arm reaching out over the water. Platon stood holding a large box.

"Here," he called to me. "Take these upstairs."

He transferred the box to my arms. I turned and struggled the heavy container of canned food up to the next level.

"One more," came the gruff voice from below.

I hoisted the box up to the next level and placed it on the floor near the cupboard.

"About damn time you woke up there, Sleepin' Beauty," Platon grumbled. "Duty time starts at sunup, Lazy Bones!"

It didn't occur to me until later that I should have asked Chip for some books as well. I made a mental note to request them next time.

Another day passed without much interaction. I tried to avoid him as much as possible, mostly staring at the meteorological instruments because I could tell he couldn't understand them.

Days passed, we emptied cans and bottles, then tossed into the unforgiving sea. Eventually, I grew to tolerate the beer beverage. Platon only spoke when absolutely necessary.

One morning he announced, "Time to clean the windows." He held out a bucket and sponge to me. Must have been the assistant's job. As dangerous as it sounded, getting some fresh, salty air might have been good for me.

After filling the bucket with water and soap powder, I descended to the mechanical level and opened the door. Like a deafening cloud, the waves crashed below me, spitting up at my feet. I took my time, pressing the soft sponge around the glass panes until I could see through them.

A metal ladder led up, and I cautiously climbed holding the bucket in one hand. At the next level, the waves distressed me less. One-by-one, I removed the built-up grime from the windows. Even with the bawl of angry ocean below, I could still hear moans from above. Perhaps Platon needed some privacy so he could read from his Bible again.

The next level proved challenging, as there was no place to stand. I had to hang onto the ladder and could only reach the windows closest to it. At the top, I could see the enormous lens through the large, curved panes. As I carefully skirted the translucent turret, I could observe the various parts of the assembly that operated the light apparatus.

Before I began this cleaning task, I approached it with dread, given the inherent danger of the breakers below lapping up with every tentacled wave. If the visibility decreased, the foghorn would begin, scaring the bejeebers out of me. However, once I reached the pinnacle of the lighthouse, I realized that a calmness had descended upon me, and I had found some serenity in something I had hitherto feared.

When the supply ship from Goat Island returned, Chip delivered a crate of soda for me. "Don't be tossing these gals out your window, Greenie. We have to take 'em back on deposit, y'know." Finally, I could have some security about not throwing things into the ocean. We stood gazing into each other's eyes for a minute or two. "You think I could put this down?" He nodded to the box in his hands.

If it were acceptable to display my affections for him, I would have walked over and kissed him full on the lips. At this stage, I still had no inclination of his inclinations. Instead, I approached him and took the crate from him, allowing our hands to rub against each other briefly. When I looked back at his face, he had a little smile too. The wooden box almost fell from my unsteady hands. He helped me place it on the floor. I reached out to touch him just as a loud whistle sounded outside.

"Gotta go. See you next month." He turned and descended. Once again I had forgotten to ask for some books.

A month, a whole month. My only consolation would be to think of him every time I put one of those soda bottles up to my lips.

As time went by, Platon interacted with me less and less. He hardly spoke, and we both went about our chores wordlessly.

Every week, I would go outside to clean the windows, whether they needed it or not. Moans above me from Platon came like clockwork in coordination with my chore.

One evening I realized only one bottle of soda remained. I had lost track of the days and hoped that the Goat Island crew, and especially Chip, would return soon.

The next day, I began my weekly window-cleaning routine as always. However, the wind had become nearly violent, the waves hungry and vociferous. As I began the ascent to the second level, my mind wandered to thoughts of the tempting and effervescent Chip. This momentary distraction allowed a stray stream of water to knock me off the ladder and into the roiling waters.

As thoughts of death overwhelmed my mind, I thrashed about helplessly, shouting for assistance. If Platon had stuck to his regular pattern, this would be his Bible-reading time, and his groans of ecstasy might mute my own calls.

Again and again, the briny cacophony sloshed me about, away from the little island and back again. With every scream, water would find its way into my mouth and down my throat. Imagining my imminent drowning blocked out almost everything else. My energy had nearly depleted when I heard a shout from above.

"Over here, Greenie!" Platon had crawled out onto the metal arm and down its chains. His hand floundered in the mist attempting to capture mine. After a few futile attempts, thwarted by the menacing movements of the sea, we finally managed to grasp one another.

With heroic strength, he pulled us both up the chain until we sat on the metal arm next to one another. In many ways, it reminded me of one of those cliff-hanger movie serials, where a handsome hero rescued the defenseless heroine from the grasps of a malevolent villain at the very last moment. Perhaps, in that instant, we more resembled Tarzan and Jane, with the not-so-handsome Platon lugging me up a well-placed jungle vine.

I heaved and coughed, making attempts to rid my lungs of the bitter seawater.

"You idiot!" he charged once I had calmed down. "Come on. Back inside." He sidled along the arm and I followed. "We better get you warm."

I followed him down to the mechanical room, where the excessive heat from the generator that usually made me sweat, felt welcome for once.

"Thank you," I finally managed to cough out. "I could have died out there."

"Yeah, I know," he said with a hint of remorse.

"I'd like to change into something else." I indicated my wet clothes. He nodded as I climbed up to the level with our cots.

As my head poked up through the floor, I noticed something unusual on Platon's cot. With casual interest, I peeked and recognized the beat-up, old Bible. It lay open with several pieces of paper scattered around it. Knowing he wouldn't be far behind, I quickly glanced and saw sketches of men in various stages of undress. I just about keeled over when I saw one of me bending over my cot!

So that's what he kept in his Bible! I had pretty much figured he couldn't read, but it turned out the book had been a hiding place for his sordid drawings. That explained quite a bit about that odd behavior and grunting. When I heard steps on the stairs below, I bolted over to my own cot and began fetching some dry clothes.

He went directly to his bed and rearranged the contents, folding some of the larger pieces before returning them to the battered book. I pretended not to notice his actions.

The rest of the day passed in silence. Neither of us mentioned either incident.

Through the evening, I kept thinking of the drawing he had made of me. When could he have had time for something like that? The man had saved my life, and I pondered its meaning. Had he taken a liking to me after all? Did I feel differently about him? Platon invaded my dreams for the first time.

In the morning, the crew from Goat Island appeared. Chip had once again provided me with a fresh crate of soda bottles. "I see you've been keeping the empties for me," he said with a bit of a grin.

I wanted to tell him that every time my lips had touched each of those bottles, I thought of kissing him full-on his full lips. "Thank you," I managed to stutter. "I… I… wanted to…"

Platon appeared seemingly out of nowhere. He glanced at me, then at Chip. A growly "Hmmmmph" emanated from his throat and he scampered up the stairs. My eyes followed his crumpled form as it disappeared above, and my heart turned slightly more in his direction.

"You were saying…?" Chip prompted me.

A heavy sigh drooped my shoulders. *Stag station*, I reminded myself. I knew what I wanted but wanted what I knew.

"Thank you," I managed to say. "I just wanted to ask you to bring me some reading books, Chip. See you next month."

"Nice Day for a Picnic"

Once again, we start at the statue in Piccadillly. This one appeared (in part) in *The Wells Street Journal*, a British literary magazine that features works about London. As it takes place in England, I have used U.K. spelling.

"Nice Day for a Picnic"

"Nice day for a picnic."

I looked up into the face of a middle-aged gentleman with noticeable sags under his steely-blue eyes made more obvious as he had bent at the waist. That toothy grin seemed amicable enough, but those mutton chops had significant amounts of grey and much of the hair on his head had previously departed.

"Beg pardon, sir?"

He straightened up and repeated his opening remark, "Nice day for a picnic."

It was May 1895. I had just received notice that my request for employment with the National Gallery had been declined–again–and news of Mr. Oscar Wilde's imprisonment brought another gloomy cloud over an otherwise gloomy day in London. The front page of *Police News* showed dramatic "Closing Scenes at the Old Bailey," and the *Evening Standard* proclaimed, "The Abominable Vices of Mr. Wilde."

My time at Oxford would soon be coming to a close and I needed to secure suitable employment. I sat upon the steps of the recently-dedicated statue of Anteros in Piccadilly pondering my fate.

The rather forward fellow bent down again and whispered in my ear, "Are you not Ajax?"

"Ajax?" I responded in a clear volume, "The Achaean? Trojan War and all that?"

"Ssshhhh! Keep your voice down, young man," he admonished. He looked left and right as if I had just revealed his secret identity to the world at large.

A moment later, a scholarly-looking gent about my age, height, hair colour and styling passed us. He sat on the stairs of the monument a few feet away.

"Excuse me. Sorry for the bother," my tormentor apologised and scooted off to the newly-arrived man. "Nice day for a picnic," he began, and the two of them chatted for a few minutes before they walked off together toward Charing Cross.

As I reflected on this odd encounter, I looked up and saw one of my old mates from Oxford. "Algie!" I called and waved. "Algie! Over here!" I stood and greeted my classmate as he stepped up from the street.

"Why you old thing! What are you doing in London?" Algernon Horatio Fitzhugh looked rather dashing in a houndstooth tweed jacket, his raven hair pomaded to the point of drowning. He was a year ahead of me at school and sat Literature.

"Oh, Algie, it's been tough. My appointment at the National Gallery fell through, and then the news of Oscar."

"Yes, poor Oscar. We're all going to have to take more care these days." He looked left and right, but I couldn't tell if it was because he was nervous about talking with me or because he was looking for someone. "It's so good to see you." He continued to swivel his head about, which led me to believe he was seeking another.

"Algie, the strangest thing just happened. An older fellow came up to me and said, 'Nice day for a picnic.'" Algie's head halted in its search. "Have you ever heard of such a thing?" He then turned his eyes on me directly. "He thought I was Ajax or some such nonsense."

Just then, another, even paunchier, middle-aged gent in a dark grey overcoat approached my friend, doffed his hat and greeted him with, "Nice day for a picnic."

My eyes bulged at the now-familiar phrase as Algie turned to the newcomer, "Yes, indeed it is. Please give us a moment, sir." He looked at me and said, "Sorry, but I've got to go." Algie reached into his jacket and pulled out a visiting card. "Here. Pay me a call, and we'll chat about the old days." With that he strode off with the very gentlemen. Indeed!

When my composure returned, I glanced at the card:

Mrs. Borden's Confidential Companions

12-13 Greek Street, London

While not familiar with that particular address, I believed it was in the area referred to as Soho, a neighbourhood well-known for its depravity.

With all the misfortune of the day, I decided it might be best to return to campus. I put Algie's card in my pocket and began walking toward the station. What kind of business could he be conducting?

In his own Oxford days, we did belong to a special boys' club, which is how we first made our acquaintance. Due to our empire's severe laws against any type of sexual relations between men, we had to be very discreet and sworn to secrecy. With the imprisonment of our Oscar, things looked to be getting even worse for men like us.

On the ride back to school, I daydreamed of languorous afternoons in the dormitory, starkers and unabashed with other like-minded fellows. We were far from home, healthy, randy young men who had biological urges that propelled us to have long sessions of sexual expression. At first, we were not sure how to satisfy each other's passions, but after a few rounds of frigging by hand together, we graduated to using our mouths and lips upon each other. Some of the boys could not acquire a taste for the semen of another, but I relished the unpredictable flavourings. Several fellows preferred to have their partners slide back-and-forth between their legs instead, kissing optional. Some of us developed forbidden feelings, as we had no other outlet for our adolescent emotions. Even at this early stage in our lives, we understood these male-to-male relationships ran counter to society at-large. The outside world had proper expectations and made unsolicited demands on our particular sex.

Not everyone chose to abide by the common rules, and some of us managed to maintain our surreptitious activities throughout the terms. I was just reminiscing about the first time I lay with Algie unrigged–and how surprising the enormity of his stiffy–as the train stopped at Oxford station. When I went to stand, I had to put a hand in front of my pants to hide the arousal caused by my reveries.

The subsequent month, once all of my classes had terminated, I traipsed back into London again for yet another disappointing round of interviews with yet more galleries. This began to worry me as my funds would evaporate after a week or so. I do not believe I was ready for the poor house just yet, especially with an Oxford degree in hand!

As I was near Tottenham Court, in Oxford Street and Charing Cross Road, I realised my proximity to the Soho neighbourhood. I pulled the card from my pocket to reacquaint myself with the address: 12-13 Greek Street.

When I reached Soho Square, I meandered along the paved paths, taking the southern way to the top of Greek Street. It seemed plain enough. Stately buildings lined the row, and I strode to the door marked 12-13. A large brass knocker in the shape of a bull's head dominated the otherwise ordinary slab of wood. I lifted the thing's head expecting it to moo or snort, but it merely created a loud "thud" when I let it free.

A moment later, the door opened a hand's-width, and a rather tall woman in a conservative, high-collar frock addressed me through the narrow gap. "May I be of assistance?" Her voice sounded somewhat deep for a woman.

"Oh, yes, please," I stammered. "I'm looking for a friend of mine who gave me this calling card." I retrieved it from my pocket and slipped the card through the opening. She snatched it from my fingers, examined it quickly and handed it back. Her expression remained placid, neither acknowledging nor denying that I was at the correct place. "His name, ma'am, is Algernon. Algernon Fitzhugh."

Her already arched eyebrows raised even higher. "I see. Well. You had better come in then, Dear Heart." She opened the door fully and walked away along a narrow entrance hall. I have been referred to as "Love," "Sir," "Master," "Mister," and "Sweetie," but never "Dear Heart."

Once inside, I could see that her manner of dress appeared quite odd. She wore neither corset nor bustle, and the puce-coloured dress seemed nearly vertical in its lines. Her chestnut hair appeared to have been plopped atop her head and knotted with a grey bow, yet it still managed to cover her ears.

She led me to a cosy sitting room with a few plush high-back chairs and a low table. Pointing her rather large hand, she indicated one of the chairs, and I sat down nervously. As I looked about the dark-panelled room, I could see stacks of ornamented china plates and cups, all in a creamy shade of light blue.

"It's Wedgwood, Dear Heart," the woman explained, "Old Josiah himself once lived here and left some of his handiwork behind. Would you care for some tea?"

When I looked into her eyes for the first time, I realised they matched the colour of the china almost exactly. "Yes, ma'am. If you please, ma'am."

She elevated her chin as if looking for stray dust on the ceiling. "Please do not call me 'ma'am.' It makes me feel rather like an old lady. Mrs. Borden is the name, if you please."

"Oh, as in Mrs. Borden's?"

"Yes, Dear Heart, the very one." She disappeared through a swinging door.

What had Algie gotten himself into? This mysterious woman, this mysterious home, this mysterious life. I just hoped he had not fallen victim to the undertow of immorality.

"Here you go, Dear Heart." Mrs. Borden returned carrying a silver-plate tea tray with two Wedgwood cups. She set it on the low table. "I've already taken the liberty of putting milk and sugar in the cup. I know how you Oxford boys like yours sweet." A hint of a smile wrinkled her face.

"How did you know I attend Oxford?"

The smile broadened. "Because of your acquaintance with young Algernon, of course." She poured from the teapot a cupful each. "I'm afraid your friend is out on business at the moment, but you're welcome to keep me company until he returns."

"Thank you. Thank you very much indeed, Mrs. Borden." I looked about the room. "Will Mr. Borden be joining us? I don't want to seem improper."

The woman's smile turned into pursed lips, "There is no Mr. Borden." She stirred using a small silver-plate spoon, which called attention to the size of her hand, especially with the pinkie extended. Two taps on the rim and she set the spoon back on the tray.

"Oh, I am truly sorry to hear that."

"No, Dear Heart," she placed the same rough, warm hand with slightly hairy knuckles upon mine. "There never *was* a Mr. Borden," and she winked at me. I wanted to pull my hand back but did not wish to seem rude to my hostess, and it remained under her cover until she finally decided to take her tea.

We sat, sipping (and it was mighty fine tea at that), without speaking.

After several minutes, she turned to me and inquired, "Do you have your affairs in order?"

"I'm not sure what it is you are asking, Mrs. Borden."

"It has come to my attention that many of the recent university graduates are having difficulties procuring positions at this time."

Given that I had just finished another set of unsatisfactory interviews, she might have been reading my mind. Or, perhaps, my face.

"Yes, Mrs. Borden, many of my schoolmates are finding it difficult to procure proper employment at this time."

"Are you one of those?" Her eyebrows arched higher again.

I decided to be candid with her because I frankly saw no advantage in prevaricating. "Yes. I had hoped that an Oxford degree would speak for itself. Up until now, it has remained rather hoarse."

She smiled a little. It could have been my slightly humorous remark or a passing thought. "I don't know if your Algernon mentioned this to you, but I do provide rooms for young men like yourself." Her eyes seemed to examine me in a watchful way similar to a job interview. Or, perhaps, an audition of some sort.

"Mrs. Borden," I set down my teacup, "while this appears to be a rather nice home, and I'm sure the rooms are top-notch, I am afraid that I could never afford the tariff, as such."

"Tariff?" She seemed surprised or taken a-back. "There is no tariff here, Dear Heart." She slurped some of her tea.

"You mean I would be able to live here without paying you anything? That seems rather generous."

She smiled and lowered her chin. "Case in point, you would earn money while you reside here."

If I had had some tea in my mouth, it might have accidentally sprayed forth like an atomiser. What kind of rooming house pays you to stay there? "Are you suggesting I become part of your house service staff, Mrs. Borden?" What else could she have been hinting at?

"No, Dear Heart. We don't have service staff here. I am proprietor, business manager and scullery maid-of-all-work rolled into one." Her tight smile hinted at courtesan flirtation.

Again I had to wonder what kind of rooming house. Oh. Wait. *That* kind of rooming house. I reminded myself we were in Soho and took some more tea straightaway. My heart raced and I could hear the pulsations in my own ear.

"We serve only the cream-of-the-cream. You would receive a percentage of the fee plus whatever gratuities your clients determine. It's all discreet and very hush-hush, you know."

"But I never —"

"No, none of us *ever*, Dear Heart, but there comes a time in a young man's life when he has to make some very difficult decisions regarding his future." Her eyes lingered on my face, searching for an answer to her unspoken query. She drummed the fingers of one hand in sequence across the side of her cheek. "Such opportunities present themselves only fleetingly." She stood and began walking to the entryway, as if preparing to usher me out to the street.

A thousand conflicting thoughts criss-crossed my mind like a train round-about at high speed. What if my parents found out? Where could something like this lead? Would this keep me from obtaining a *bona fide* position? When would I receive an honest job offer? How would I be able to pay for my next meal? "Wait!" I blurted. Mrs. Borden returned to the chair. "Would I have to be… you know… um… intimate… with these gentlemen?"

"Why, Dear Heart, what do you think this is, a brothel?"

I looked around the rather comfortably-appointed room, with its dark, plush furniture, china rails, mahogany highboy, and ivory statuettes. A bit of butter-upon-bacon, if you ask me. Yes, it did give one the air of a bordello.

"Well, I can see where one might arrive at the incorrect impression; however, no intimacy–as you put it–occurs here under my roof. If a gentleman wishes a thruppenny-upright, he can find that sort of thing in Gropecunt Lane." She pointed in a generally westward direction. "And, besides, if that's all he wants: he's no gentlemen. I only provide companions for the well-to-do: MPs, titled nobles, and the sort." Her face shifted to a self-satisfied sneer. "My clients are select, discreet, and proper."

"I must confess, Mrs. Borden, given the recent bad turn for Mr. Wilde we must all be cautious with our affairs, and I am currently attempting to procure proper employment with a local gallery."

"My boys are all university-educated and well-bred. No laws are broken; although, some might be temporarily bent." She giggled to herself. "As it so happens, I have a vacancy at this time. You shall be taken care of very well, and you can still pursue your scholarly interests."

As if responding to a cue line from a play script, my midsection grumbled its desire for nourishment.

Mrs. Borden's eyes grew big and she focused on my abdomen. "It sounds like at least one part of you is interested." She stood and disappeared through the swinging door again, this time returning with a small tray of biscuits. As she held the assortment just below my chin, I could see my reflection in the polished metal. My face appeared narrower than the last time I had looked. The purse in my pocket was not the only thing growing thin.

I snatched up a sweet, trying to be nonchalant about my hunger, although I suspected Mrs. Borden knew more than she had let on. "Would you like to stay on, then? Anyone Algernon vouches for is welcome here."

In my mind I saw Algie's naked body and wished he could comfort me in this black hour. I felt a bit poked up but swallowed the biscuit with a tight gulp. "Yes," I sobbed. "Yes, yes."

There are worse ways to earn one's living, I suppose, and most of us must prostitute ourselves some time, some way, or another.

A knock at the door prompted Mrs. Borden to rise. "Just a moment," she shouted toward the front. "Make yourself comfortable, Dear Heart." Easier said than done. Left alone in this gaudy chamber, my thoughts raced again. How could I explain such a situation to my parents? *Yes, mum and dad, I am rooming with me ol' chuckaboo Algie from uni. No, I haven't managed to secure a solid position yet. How can I afford to pay for the room? Well, it's a bit of a sticky story, but...*

Mrs. Borden returned with a lanky fellow dressed in all black. His grey hair appeared matted down, as if he had recently been sporting a periwig. Pink cheeks and a pinched nose framed his narrow mouth. His eyes seemed locked upon me. I stood as they entered.

"Well, aren't you the jammiest bit of jam?" he squealed in a high-pitched tone. Now, there's a phrase I have not heard in many a-year.

"Now, now," tutted Mrs. Borden, "This one is not part of my crew... at least not just yet." She indicated one of the other chairs. "Come. Sit. I'll bring you the catalogue."

As the gentleman seated himself, Mrs. Borden retrieved a picture album from the green marble mantle and handed it to him. She and I observed his perusing through the book. It appeared to contain photographs of young men about my age pasted on each page. On one of the leaves I saw Algie's picture with the name "Achilles" written underneath. When I looked at the other names, they all had some reference to Greek history or mythology. That would explain "Ajax," whose likeness, on the following page, matched the other fellow at the fountain that day the previous month. I could see how a person could mistake the two of us.

After a minute or so, the caller turned back a few pages and pointed to the picture of "Ajax" and smiled at Mrs. Borden, then at me.

"Oh, no, your lordship. That is not him. Ajax is another. When would you desire his company?"

His lordship's smile drooped at the news. "This afternoon, if possible, at half past five."

Mrs. Borden stood, took the picture book and returned it to the mantle. "Of course, your lordship. Have past five it is." She held out her hand, palm up, and smiled at the gentleman.

With one more longing look at me, he stood and thrust his right hand into his pants pocket. In his fist appeared a wad of banknotes, from which he peeled a few and placed them in Mrs. Borden's upturned hand. She gave them a cursory counting and smiled. The notes disappeared into a hidden pocket of her skirt, and she led the caller out.

I sat again, taking in the splendour of the parlour.

"You see, Dear Heart," Mrs. Borden explained as she approached, "that is how we conduct our business. As long as no illegal acts are performed under my roof, I remain a citizen in good-standing."

The situation became clear. The clients come here to make their selection, and then meet their companion elsewhere, presumably the statue in Piccadilly.

"Nice day for a picnic?" I queried.

"What, Dear Heart?"

"Nice day for a picnic. That's the phrase the gentleman would use when meeting his chosen companion."

"Why, yes," she blinked. "You are the quick study, aren't you now?"

I related my experience from the previous month. "And that's when I became reacquainted with Algernon."

"Of course. When do you expect to be taking the room, Dear Heart?" Her eyes questioned me.

"If I may ask, Mrs. Borden, what is expected of these companions? You say no illegal acts transpire, but my curiosity is getting the better of me, I'm afraid."

"Ah. You wish to know the nature of our business." She sat, crossing her ankles purposefully. "Well, each client has different… needs, shall we say, and you merely follow his direction." The blank look on my face must have communicated my lack of understanding. "These gentlemen require certain… acts, as it were, to provide for their personal entertainment." She winked at me, which I took as a suggestion of sexual favours.

"But are we required to have carnal relations with the customers?"

"Heavens, no!" She drew a hand to her mouth. "As I maintain, my staff provide companionship, nothing more. If any of my clients–and that's how we refer to them, not customers–imposes any act of a sexual nature, they are no longer my client. I am quite firm on that." Her eyebrows raised high again.

That was comforting to know because I did not think I could work up any physical interest in these older, tweedle-dum chaps. "And then exactly what services do we provide, Mrs. Borden?"

"Your client may take you to dine, to a pub, perhaps to a hotel room. Many of them like to play what we call 'games'."

"Games? Like draughts or chess?"

"No, no," she chuckled, "these games employ very little strategy, and I believe you will learn quickly just how easy –"

The door opened and Algie came in. "Algie!" I cried as I stood. He rushed up to hug me. "Or should I be calling you Achilles?" My grin felt impetuous.

"Oh, I see Mrs. Borden has wasted no time showing you the catalogue." Light glistened off his shiny hair.

"No, Dear Heart, a client stopped by." I am relieved to hear that I am not the only one whom she calls Dear Heart. "Why don't you and your friend go up to your room. You can catch him up on how things work around here."

"Yes! Let's!" Algie responded enthusiastically. He grasped my open hand and led me to a narrow set of stairs.

"Thank you, Mrs. Borden," I shouted as I followed him up.

Over the next hour I explained how downhearted I had become, seeming to be shooting into the brown more times than would be predicted for someone with my background. The economy seemed to have soured, and I, merely a victim of circumstances.

Algie told me how the various clients like to play dress-up and pretend. Most of it sounded very schoolyard, but if that's what they want to pay us for, like every other red-blooded British boy, I've done my time on the boards and can do Thespis reasonably well. My portrayal of Puck in *A Midsummer's Night Dream* drew much attention during my salad days.

He showed me my room, and I asked him to stay the night, but he explained that Mrs. Borden does not permit such fraternizing. That left me holding my own tallywag, as it were.

In the morning, Mrs. Borden accompanied me to the photographer's studio down the lane. He snapped a few of my head and shoulders, similar to the pictures in the catalogue.

As we walked back, Mrs. Borden inquired, "Have you thought of your companion name yet?"

I hadn't given it much thought, if truth be known. Most of the good ones had already been chosen. However, one obvious name stood out to me. "Hermes," I stated. "I believe Hermes might suit."

She smiled in satisfaction. "Indeed it does."

Over the next week, I began to settle in at Mrs. Borden's, and requests for my companionship ensued. At first I had so much hesitation about going with unfamiliar men, but with Mrs. Borden's assurances that all the gentlemen were, in fact, gentlemen, plus Algie's reassurances, I launched my career as a well-paid bunter.

The first time caused the most stress. Unaware of the "games" these gentlemen liked to indulge in, it quickly became evident to me that they were most harmless and far from illegal. We never touched in a sexual way, it was all make-believe and fairy stories. My first gentlemen merely wanted me to watch him prance around while he got made up like a French chambermaid. I never! Then he requested me to command him and provide harsh punishment should he not behave properly. He certainly seemed after wanting the punishment.

A few days later, the tall, "jammiest bit of jam" fellow I had met on my first day requested my services. He was a queer one. We sat in his drawing room together while he fiddled beneath a blanket he had thrown over his lap.

Then there was the peculiar Lord Q. He did not meet me at the steps of the statue in Piccadilly; he sent a manservant to fetch me. At one point a few blocks away, the servant required me to wear a blindfold so that I could not determine the location of Lord Q's home. Once inside, I was led to a darkened room and the blindfold removed. Across from me stood a grey fabric triptych.

From behind the panels a voice emerged. "Turn round. Thank you. Please sit on the stool behind you."

I did as commanded. Hearing no further orders, I merely sat and waited, attempting to make sense of this small, dark chamber.

A few minutes later the voice called out again. "All right. You may go now."

The manservant reappeared, reapplied the blindfold and led me back to the spot where he had first saddled me with the black cloth. Before I could take two steps, the servant grabbed me by the left wrist, turned me about and placed a few bank notes in my right hand. I smiled and swiftly placed the notes in my pocket before any street thieves could take notice.

Back at Mrs. Borden's, in the safety of my chamber, I took the wad of paper from my pants to find two one-pound notes and a scrap of paper, on which was written: "I shall see you again."

I didn't give much thought to this episode until Lord Q's manservant met me again in Piccadilly the following week. Just like last time, he blindfolded me, led me to the small chamber, where I sat for a few minutes longer this time, and got led back to the initial spot. My reward turned out to be three quid and a similar "see you again" message.

This went on for a few months. Each time, the duration increased, and I began to fantasize what the elusive Lord Q might look like—and just what he might be doing behind the grey screens. How hideous he must be if he needed to secrete himself.

During these weeks I continued—rather unsuccessfully, I must confess—to apply myself at galleries for work in my field of study. It seemed all my studies were for naught.

One day in late summer, while in Lord Q's chamber, I decided to alter the procedure. While sitting on the stool, I stared at the triptych, something I had not done previously. Most of my previous stool-bound time went to mentally reviewing the events of my last disappointing job interview or wishing there were a window to peer out. As I concentrated on the grey fabric across the room, I could hear heavy breathing, something I had not encountered previously. This unexpected development aroused me, and I soon had a somewhat conspicuous stiffy to contend with. I reached into my pocket to rearrange my bits as had they gotten scrambled, and I could hear the respiration intensify. The triptych began to wobble and I feared it might regrettably fall, revealing the monstrous Lord Q in all his disagreeable nature.

All of a moment, the panels toppled toward me to display a handsome, youthful gentleman, perhaps a few years older than me, sitting in a leather reading chair. His pink face flushed bright red, his shoulder regions pink as a pig, and a mountain of blond curls wriggled uncontrollably about his head. All contrasted against the dark material behind him. A gasp bolted from his mouth just as a pearly shower flew across the chamber at me, some of which splashed my face. The taste of his salty juices on my tongue enflamed my desires.

Lord Q rushed to me and kissed my mouth in a way I had never faced before. He plunged his dart-like tongue between my lips and it was now my turn to experience the agony of bliss. Within my own breeches, I exploded like an artillery barrage.

He stepped back, and we just studied each other's face for a few minutes. We had just committed a punishable offense in the eyes of the law.

"I am truly sorry," he began, "I did not intend to involve you in my crime of passion." He stepped to his chair and retrieved a dressing gown from behind it. "When I saw your photo in the catalogue I knew that I wanted you, but I had to be ever so cautious."

I nodded in agreement, stunned by what had just transpired between us. If he were a government official, Lord Q might turn me over to the police and that would be the end of my career.

"Mrs. Borden was so kind as to explain your particular financial situation, and I have something of an offer to propose to you." He sat in the chair, facing me. "I possess a rather large collection of works passed down through my family: paintings, sculptures and the like. If truth be told, I could use someone with your background to curate my things. It would entail you taking a room here with me." His smile revealed that there might be some other handiwork around the manor as well.

Well dash my wig! Finally, a successful job interview. A position with many, many benefits, particularly in this time of persecution for people who engage in Mr. Wilde's "love that dare not speak its name." Being in the service of Lord Q provided certain protections not afforded elsewhere. I finally took the egg I had so tirelessly pursued.

I shall not reveal my Lord's identity, nor where his house stood. We lived together, enjoyed each other's company as best we could, and through the years we became as close as any married couple might.

With no family or offspring, he made me his sole heir. Upon his death in May 1914, I took possession of the house and his collection of well-curated art. The manor soon seemed empty and cold, and I decided upon a satisfying solution.

On a bright spring afternoon, nearly 20 years since the day I first sat upon the pedestal of the Anteros statue in Piccadilly, the *Evening Herald* proclaims, "Assassination May Lead to War." As I approach the sculpture I can see a young man–who rather reminds me of old Algie–seated upon the second tier of concrete steps. I step up to him and say, "Nice day for a picnic."

Noah's Raft

Originally written as a submission for *Best Gay Erotica of the Year* calling for stories set in olden times (rejected because it did not contain enough sex), it eventually made it into *Off the Rocks* in their tribute to history.

Noah's Raft

Diary Entry:

April 7, 1865

Worked in front garden. Raided Arsenal with ANJ.
Booty obtained, no injuries. Quota fuifilled. Will work
with Smythe tomorrow to secure raft.

The Real Story:

I heard a minie ball whiz past my right ear as I ran from the armory. From the sound of the gun and the projectile's hum, I would have presumed it was a Remington 1858, standard Union Army issue.

Trying to skedaddle in the dark with a 25-pound box of ammunition under my arm was quite challenging enough, but at the same time I had to draw my weapon, determine my target behind me, pray that my somewhat unreliable Colt would function properly, and fire thusly. I could only hope I had the skills and experience to do just that.

Because I am a bit shorter than the preponderance of adult men, the bullets tend to fly above my head, most of the time. This one almost nicked my ear, even though I was running down the hill of Jefferson Street, one of my namesakes, as it so happened.

The soldier catching up to me wore those noisy Union Army boots, and that enabled me to locate him precisely. While I do not relish the killing of another human being, even if he is a Yankee Devil, I must do what I need to do to accomplish my mission.

Just as another bullet passed near my head, I stopped briefly, turned about, and raised my gun to the angle where I could disable the bastard by shooting him just above the top of the boot leather, approximately 15 inches from the ground. Praise be to the Glory of Heaven, my Colt fired when I squeezed the trigger, and a second later I heard a scream of agony and a thump.

I started running again, turning onto Military Way and back toward Noah's house at East Second and J Streets. I had lost sight of him but trusted we would meet back at home.

Before I go on, allow me the honor of introducing myself. Born Beauregard Jefferson Lee (no relation to our esteemed military commander), I usually go by just my initials: BJ. A few months before the outbreak of this horrible War Between the States, I had signed up to ride for the Pony Express, helping to deliver the mail satchels. They required men of smaller stature, and due to providence, I was short enough and light enough to meet their standard. It was the first time in my life that being petite had worked in my favor.

My route took me back and forth from Placerville, California, to Carson City, in Nevada Territory. One day in April 1861, I pulled into Placerville ready to hand off the mochila, the specially-designed mail pouch. However, my supervisor informed me that one of the Nevada Territory riders had been ambushed by Paiutes, and we were short couriers. He requested I ride on to Sacramento and complete the delivery.

After refreshing myself, I headed out. When I finally arrived in Sacramento, the steamship that normally took the mail on to San Francisco had already set sail, and I was required to ride down to the port of Benicia, where another ship would take the mochila.

Exhausted after my extended ride, I handed off the mail to the supervisor at Solano Hotel on First and E Streets and booked a room for the night. In the lobby I saw a handbill for the Knights of the Golden Circle, a gentleman's society I had frequented back home in Virginia. Being a stranger in the town, I attended the gathering that evening in the hope of meeting other, like-minded fellows.

Down a block, at the Union Hotel (which I later found humorously, and ironically, named), in a meeting room off the lobby, cigar smoke clouded the warm spring air to the point I could barely make out others in the room. I did not partake of the Devil's weed, but it did not offend me if others did so.

When I sat, to my right was a most handsome chap, whose name I later found out was Abraham Noah Jones. Tall, swarthy, muscular. All the things I was not. I had my long reddish hair tied behind my head the way our celebrated Thomas Jefferson wore his. Noah (as he preferred to be called) kept his black, wavy locks shorter, but they still managed to curl into small ringlets at the end.

The meeting was led by a fellow with the assumed name of Colonel Smythe, who spoke eloquently, like a Philadelphia lawyer, about the need to maintain the current economic status by means of Negro labor.

I, myself, did not own any slaves. I found the idea of possessing another human being repulsive, but I understood the need to keep the wheels of business moving forward. This Colonel Smythe did not specifically advocate the violent overthrow of the government (for that is against the Constitution), but he certainly riled up the men in the room to stand for the right to maintain slavery. The group appeared to be populated with displaced Southerners and Copperhead sympathizers.

Following the meeting, Mr. Jones turned to me and asked if I was visiting "B'nisha." I told him I did not understand what he meant. He laughed playfully and told me that Benicia is pronounced "Buh-NEE-shuh" by the Mexicans and "Buh-NISH-uh" by the White People. I told him I was a Pony Express rider, and he invited me to stay with him at his home nearby. While he seemed to take a cotton to me, and I certainly found him most appealing, I told him I would probably be staying just the one night, leaving early the next morning. He bowed graciously and bid me a good evening.

What I did not tell the stunning Mr. Jones was how much he reminded me of a childhood friend back in Culpeper. Zachary was also tall, slender and dark. We would tussle around down near the fishing creek, and one day he accidentally brushed up against my firm adolescence. He smiled sheepishly, took my hand and placed it upon his own hardness. We looked around to see if anyone else was within hollering distance, and finding no one, we proceeded to satisfy our young, male urges with one another. This continued for a few months until Zachary decided (or, more likely, someone else decided for him) it was no longer proper to have that sort of relationship.

Following the K.G.C. meeting, I walked out First Street to the shore along the San Francisco Bay. I could barely make out the tip of the next town over, Vallejo, as it poked out into the Carquinez Strait. When I returned to the Solano Hotel, the bar was full of rowdies and fancy girls who worked on the second floor, attempting to ply their charms on patrons who desired such horizontal refreshments.

The next morning, newspaper headlines declared a state of war. Rebels had fired upon the nearly-completed Fort Sumter in Charleston Harbor. The moment we all dreaded had finally arrived. The rumors proved true, and our great nation was about to have its foundation in democracy tested.

The Pony Express supervisor came to me and explained that my services would no longer be required because the routes were not secure due to the outbreak of war. Here I was, thousands of miles from my home, no job, no friends. There were leather tanneries and breweries in town, but that was not the kind of work I was designed for. My slight frame was more suited to operations that did not require muscles and sinew.

I decided to breakfast down at the Union Hotel. Colonel Smythe's group had already gathered in the lobby. "Mr. Lee," I heard someone call out, "Mr. Lee. I had hoped I would see you again."

It was the dashing Mr. Jones I had met the prior evening at the K.G.C. rally. "Mr. Lee, when I heard about the situation in the East, I thought you might be without a job or a home. Am I correct in that?"

I nodded sadly to the truth.

"Then it is it fate, indeed, for us both." I glanced up at his slightly mischievous smile. "My handyman has departed to fight with the Army and I need someone to assist me with the chores." He winked at me, and I was beginning to get the idea that "chores" might involve more than fixing broken fences and scuttling coal. In fact, I would have been surprised if there had even been a handyman at all.

Diary Entry:

April 8, 1865

Sowed back garden with vegetables. Dinner at von Pfister's. Smythe requested more booty. Raided Arsenal with ANJ again. More soldiers but booty still obtained. Both slightly injured. Tomorrow we secure the raft.

The Real Story:

After last night's raid, the armory was more closely guarded. Instead of one lonely watchman, three unlucky privates stood guard. Noah and I devised a ruse to draw them away from the munitions storehouse. He would walk past and engage them in distracting conversation while I slipped into the depository to gather the necessary arms.

If he had stuck to the original plan it might have gone as we had designed, but he let his vainglorious sense of pride get away with him, and he felt it his duty and obligation to verbally defend the Confederate States of America single-handedly to three Union soldiers on a U.S. Army base. Thank goodness he is very handsome.

Instead of misdirecting their attention, Noah managed to arouse their suspicion. I was just sneaking out the door with another case of ammunition when one of the boys in blue spotted me. He alerted his comrades and the chase was on again. I ran down Jefferson Street as I had last night. However, this time three Remingtons shot at me instead of just the one.

For all his appeal, Noah is not a good shot, and his aim was a sin to Crockett. In fact, I believe the noise and smell of the powder do scare him. I could hear a few clicks and shots from the Colt I had given him, but it sounded like some of those got closer to me than the ones from the Union men. One of the bullets, and I am not certain which, grazed the arm I used for holding the wooden crate. I wanted to fire back at the Yankees but was afraid I might hit Noah on accident.

Just as I approached Military Way, I heard one shot go in the opposite direction. "Ow! Blazes!" shouted Noah, and I knew what had happened. It pained me to do so, but I continued on back to East Second Street. We were committed to the cause, and if it meant the loss of one man, then we had to accept that eventuality. Even though Noah had been discharged from the Naval Academy, he had successfully managed his family's Kentucky tobacco plantation for many years, and I would just have to rely on his ability to rescue himself tonight.

When I got back to Noah's, I set down the box of ammunition then quickly stripped off the jacket and shirt to see what the damage was. Fortunately, the projectile only removed a few layers of skin from my forearm, nothing more. Yet still it burned like a hot poker, and I needed to cleanse the wound. After I poured alcohol into a rag and doused the raw flesh, my screams of pain did not even closely approach the emotional turmoil I felt over the possible loss of my darling Noah.

About 15 minutes later, I heard the door latch and grabbed my gun, just in case. The footsteps sounded like Noah, but I held my weapon until I saw him enter the room. His right sleeve showed blood flow, and I put the gun down and rushed to him.

"I'm all right, BJ. Just a little flesh wound, nothing more." He hugged me with the left arm and managed to remove his jacket on his own, which I took as a good sign. However, once he had removed his shirt, I could see that his wound was deeper and dirtier than mine had been. He looked down at the blackened flesh and promptly fainted.

Taking advantage of the situation, I cleaned his wound. Thank the heavens he was unconscious because had the rascal been awake, he would have been bawling like a banshee. Just as I finished tying the clean bandage around his arm, he roused.

"One of the minor inconveniences of war, BJ, my little possum." Looking up at me from the floor, he smiled that disarming smile of his and puckered his lips. Thinking to myself, that was the kind of behavior that probably got him expelled from Annapolis, I leaned over and kissed him. "Did you get hurt?" He glanced at my arm. I explained the superficiality of the wound and he reached up to hug me.

Our sexual congress occurred with some regular frequency, but this evening it was sufficient for me that neither of us got seriously hurt during the course of the raid. Apparently the wound upon Noah's arm did not deter his manhood from rising to the occasion. Noah is more aggressive than me about such things. He kissed me again ardently and then pulled me down to the floor. Along the way he managed to undo my britches, sliding the rough fabric down my short legs. His big, warm hands caressed my thighs, and with one practiced tug, my drawers disappeared.

His next motion was to remove his own clothing while holding his legs with his hands. The one arm still painful, he was only able to keep the other leg lifted for our enjoyment. Even though Noah was taller and stronger, it was his preference to have me bugger him. Fortunately, a jar of grease was within my arm's reach and I prepared myself. People naturally assume that my small stature indicates a similar-proportioned male organ. Noah was quite pleasantly surprised to find me an exception to that particular presumption. Every time he saw me unclothed, he would say, "Such a gigantic gun for such a small soldier!"

Because of my slightly-larger organ, the first few times we tried this it took a while before he could relax enough for me to complete the penetration. Now, after a few years, Noah could accommodate me without a much of a hitch.

The moist, warm sensation felt so good that I had to struggle to keep from jumping the hedge too soon. This was one pleasure I did not wish to deny myself. Unbidden thoughts about the upcoming mission strayed into my head, distracting but helpful. Even so, tonight was different somehow. After being together for a few years we had become almost mechanical in our love making, but in this intense moment it was as if it were the last time we would ever be together. More kissing, more hugging, more eye contact, more affection. I did not know if it was the excitement of our escapade, the anticipation of tomorrow, or some other impenetrable reason. Even though he was unable to use one arm, Noah still managed to finish with his usual fireworks. I gazed upon his adorable face, his crystal blue eyes, allowed the inevitable release and collapsed on top of him. We held on to each other in a sloppy heap and stayed like that, kissing and chatting, for quite a while.

It probably goes without saying, but after my first night in Benicia back in 1861, I ended up moving in with Noah. He took care of all my needs, and I helped him with keeping his home in good order.

We regularly attended the K.G.C. meetings at von Pfister's, an old adobe pub off First Street, preparing ourselves for the eventual Confederate invasion of California. Our group meetings had moved from the Union Hotel after the commencement of the War. Last week word finally arrived that our clandestine unit was being called into action.

A courier was on his way from Richmond with a Letter of Marque signed by none other than President Jefferson Davis, giving us the right to privateer for the C.S.A. All we needed was a ship. Noah and I had been assigned to obtain ammunition for the guns, and all last week we retrieved one crate a night. We possessed plenty of ordinance now and had every piece of equipment we needed, save the vessel to sail upon.

At this evening's meeting, prior to the Arsenal raid, Colonel Smythe informed us the courier was one day away. We were to commandeer a clipper ship moored at the Mare Island Naval Ship Yard. The *Syren* was in dock once again for repair, and it would be easy prey for our small band. Its superior speed would aid us in privateering and also in escape.

During our walk home after the meeting Noah and I discussed how much we enjoyed our life together, at home and in the service of our homeland far away. After years of plotting and waiting, we were about to spring into action.

Diary Entry:

April 9, 1865

Slept most of the day. Worked in the back garden. Dinner at von Pfister's. Mission begins.

The Real Story:

At dinner, Colonel Smythe presented the Letter of Marque from President Jefferson Davis. It named my dearest Noah Honorary Commander Jones of the *C.S.S. Uranian*, which I had hoped was a reference to the steamer ship similarly named *Mars* and not a reference to my Honorary Commander's particular predilection for gentlemen. Upon commandeering the *Syren*, it would be christened thusly.

The Colonel assigned me, Noah and four other members to take command of the clipper ship docked over in Vallejo. In addition, he had word that the Union Treasury ship *Shubrick* sat ready at Yerba Buena Cove, Port of San Francisco, to convey a shipment of gold coins to Panama for transport back to Washington.

At this time, the Confederacy was nearly bankrupted, both in spirit and in resources. If we could capture this gold shipment and turn it over to the C.S.A., we would be heroes.

When we checked the tidal charts, they showed high tide would occur at 2:31 a.m. That meant the *Shubrick* could not sail out the Golden Gate until the flow of the Bay went in the same direction. We wanted to have the best advantage, and that meant attempting to capture her by 1:00, well before the entire compliment was onboard.

We discussed strategy while eating and, after we had all finished our food, headed down to the foot of First Street where a skiff waited for us. Noah and I sat at the prow while the other four men rowed us across Glen Cove and then the mouth of the Napa River. The nearly-full moon rose over the hills and provided us with light bouncing off the glimmering little waves. As we turned upriver, we could see the tall masts of the *Syren* off to the left. Because the tide was with us, it did not take long to arrive at our prey.

From our low position, we could not determine how many sailors guarded the vessel. As it was in for repairs, we hoped the number would be less than six. Noah instructed the oarsmen to put us in at the next dock. The men secured the skiff and we hopped ashore as quietly as we could. The wooden timbers of the larger ship squawked with each pulse of the tide, helping to cover the noise of our footfalls.

Noah sent one of the men up the gangplank to reconnoiter. Upon his return, we learned there were only four men on deck, and two of them appeared to be sleeping. Our Honorary Commander instructed us not to shoot unless it was a matter of life and death. We were to strike the patrol unconscious with the Colts, using them as cudgels because they were almost useless as guns.

In single file, we crept up the plank, attempting to make as little noise as possible. When the first man reached the rail, he looked over, turned back to us waving his arm to indicate an advance. We all charged up onto the deck. Our first two men bludgeoned the patrolling sailors. When the sleeping men awoke, the other two of our gang grabbed them and threw them overboard while Noah and I assisted getting the unconscious sailors down the gangplank.

Back onboard, Noah took command of the vessel, claiming it in the name of the Confederate States of America. Two of the men pried off the nameplates, and the other two removed the U.S. flag from its mounting, dropping it into the cold water below. We had not thought to bring a Confederate flag with us, and we would have to sail without a standard.

From the quarterdeck, Noah gave the orders to weigh anchor and shove off. Our crew unfurled a few of the sails to get us moving. By the time we were in open waters, it was just about eleven o'clock. We would now be sailing against the tide, but the clipper ship proved to be a bit faster than we had expected.

As we approached Yerba Buena Cove, we could see the *Shubrick* tied up at Central Wharf. It was close to 1:00. The rigging of the Treasury ship was still lashed, which meant it would be a while before the ship was going anywhere. Our best hope was that we arrived after the cargo had been laded and before the entire complement came aboard. Through the spyglass, I could not see anyone moving about, but I was quite certain there had to be a small unit of Union sailors guarding the precious strongboxes of gold coins.

We pulled up to the same wharf but on the opposite side and dropped anchor. Noah ordered the placement of the gangplank and we marched down quietly, guns drawn in the event of confrontation. Our scout stealthily clambered up the *Shubrick*'s plank and peered over the rail. He crept back down to report one sailor standing guard, most likely the first mate. He could only see a few others nearby, but no one appeared to be at the ready for battle.

"Follow me, men," Noah whispered. He strode up the plank and stepped onto the deck. I could see the first mate and two other sailors standing close by. Noah reached into his coat and pulled out the Letter of Marque from Jefferson Davis. "I am Commander Jones of the Confederate vessel *Uranian*," he proclaimed, "and under the terms of this Letter of Marque, I claim this vessel for—"

Before he could finish the sentence, the first mate had drawn a pistol and shot Noah three times in the chest. I stood transfixed as I watched my lover crumple backwards into a pile on the deck. My nerves fired explosively and I reached for my own Colt. When I pulled the trigger, all I got was a click.

With all the rage of a mother bear, I leapt upon the Yankee who had killed my Noah. His Remington slid about a foot away, and I picked it up, firing over and over into his ugly Mudsill face. After three shots, the empty barrel did nothing but click. When I realized there were no more bullets, I turned the gun about and used it as a bludgeon, slapping it against his head, left then right, again and again. The hot barrel burned my hand, but I did not care about my own pain at that point.

I felt a hand on my shoulder. I looked up into my comrade's face. He just shook his head from side-to-side, indicating that the fellow was dead and there was no further need to continue my emotional and futile attack.

When I looked about, I could see the other Union sailors unconscious, blindfolded and tied. I moved to Noah, lifeless and pale. I hugged his empty shell tightly until I felt another tap on the shoulder. The body felt very heavy when I attempted to lift him. The other men assisted me to get him back to the *Uranian*.

Even though my anger blazed, I suppressed it in order to complete the assigned mission. The five of us remaining re-boarded the *Shubrick* and searched for the boxes of coins. We found five crates in the hold bearing the seal of the U.S. Treasury. Four of the boxes weighed about 50 pounds, but one was a bit bigger and heavier than the others. It took us three trips to get all five boxes aboard the *Uranian*, but we eventually finished around half past one, the time when the rest of the crew would probably begin to arrive.

Just as we untied our ship's mooring and weighed the anchor, I could see people climbing onto the *Shubrick*. Within seconds, raised voices screamed questions and spat orders. By then we were nearly out of gun range, but it didn't matter because none of their artillery had been at the ready anyway.

As the tide had not yet turned, our speed was better than the voyage west. Besides, we had the advantage of having the faster vessel should they decide to pursue us. From their inaction, it seemed the rest of the crew had no idea what cargo they were supposed to be transporting.

A few minutes later we heard the boom of a few cannons. The water about 100 yards behind us splashed hungrily with the striking of the ineffectual cannon balls.

It was nearly 3:00 when the dock at the end of First Street came into view. We moored the craft but did not lower a plank. Our plan was to remain onboard until morning. We did not want to leave the booty unattended, nor did I want to leave Noah.

Diary Entry:

April 10, 1865

Commandeered raft. Crossed pond. Acquired coins. Finders' keepers. Lost ANJ. Lost CSA. At sea.

The Real Story:

When the gloomy sun rose following the night of our heroic adventure, I was still mourning the loss of my dearest companion, Noah. Because I had no right to his home, and he had no relatives that I knew of, we decided to take his body into the house and leave a note for the local authorities. I had thought about burying him in the garden, but then realized I wanted someone to find him and provide the proper care. One of the men assisted me in getting his unwieldy body onto a cart, up First Street, into his house and up the stairs to the bedroom. By then he was cold as a wagon tire. We lifted him onto the bed and arranged his body as best we could. I asked my comrade to leave the room, saying I would meet him downstairs in a few minutes.

My last few moments with Noah–or his lifeless figure, more precisely–allowed me to reminisce about our chance meeting, the friendship and love that had developed between us and the life we had shared in this quirky port town. I gave him one last hug, a dry kiss on the cheek, a salute, and a hopeless smile.

I scrawled a quick message requesting that someone go to Noah's home to take care of him. One tear dripped down my face and moistened the paper. I sniffled and wiped at my eyes.

Along the way back to the *Uranian*, we happened to pass by the Union Hotel where a large celebratory boodle poured out into First Street. A broadside posted on the wall read: "Great! Grand! Glorious! The Death Blow of the Rebellion! Surrender of General Lee and his Entire Army!" As it turned out, the Confederacy as we knew it had ended the previous day, but we had no word until this morning. Our nocturnal mission turned out to be for naught. We had risked our lives for our precious country, which no longer ex-isted. I stepped into the Hotel, placed the note on the desk and quickly departed.

Back onboard, we explained the news to the rest of our posse. The way we saw it, we stood on a stolen vessel holding stolen gold. If any Union authority caught us, we would probably spend the rest of our lives in a federal prison as co-conspirators to grand larceny.

After a short discussion, we decided to sail our boat out into open waters as quickly as possible in hopes that no one would take notice. It seemed now a good thing that we did not hoist a Stars and Bars banner. We had no supplies with us, but once we had safely passed out of the Golden Gate, we could stop at some coastal town.

Even though the caskets of coins were treasury strongboxes, it did not take us long to make short work of them with small tools we found onboard. I certainly used my anger and frustration to the best advantage. The smaller boxes contained approximately a thousand $10 gold pieces each. The larger box held $20 double eagles. The rest of the crew voted to give me the larger cache because of my association with Noah.

After we cleared Fort Point, we headed south and put in at Spanishtown, about 30 miles south of the Presidio. Using some of our purloined money, we purchased enough supplies for a month's voyage.

Back aboard the *Uranian*, the other men and I discussed where we should head. It seemed obvious soon enough we no longer had an actual home to return to, and the consensus was just to see where the tides and the winds propelled us. Even though

Jefferson Davis himself had chosen the name for our new home upon the sea, I shall always consider it Noah's Raft.

Sunday/Sinday

This is the newest addition to the collection. Not written for a submission, the prompts for this involve things I saw on television. One was a fleeting ad for a sporting event, and the other was a recreation of an episode from a 1970s sitcom, *All in the Family*. Sometimes, the oddest things become stories.

Sunday/Sinday

"The Lord shall rain fire and brimstone down upon those of you who stray from His path!" The Reverend John Dickson's equally fiery eyes glowered at the congregation assembled around me. A splinter from the old wooden pew began to burrow into my bottom.

It had been years since I attended worship. When my father died on Breed's Hill eight years ago defending the Crown, my belief in a supreme being dissipated. As Loyalists, we had few interactions with other residents in our little town of Swampscott. Nonetheless, my mother continued attending this church. Given her recent demise, I had even less use for an invisible, all-seeing creator. However, as it was her funeral service, it might have appeared cruel if I had not attended.

The reverend pointed a slender finger at various others in the small church. "You... and you..."–the focus of his gaze and index digit fell directly upon me–"and you!" His eyes softened and his brow dropped. A brief pause and slight head tilt gave me the idea he recognized me in a way other than as my departed mother's son. "And you!" he continued to accuse those around me.

Following the service, he approached as I made an attempt to put some distance between me and the cold, stone building I had just exited. "Mr. Constant! Azariah!" he called out.

"Yes, Reverend," I responded once I had halted and turned to face him, the bright, yellow sky behind him fashioning a silhouette.

He blinked a few times then reached out to take my hand. It felt warm and slightly moist. "How good to see you. My heartiest lamentations over the passing of your dear mother."

"Thank you, Reverend. Your sermon was most…"–I realized he still held my hand and pulled it away–"invigorating." We did not share religious beliefs, but I thought it best to say something appreciative.

"May I ask you something?" He caught my arm as I passed.

His grasp drew my attention. "Of course."

"I could not help but notice you are not crying. If that had been my mother who passed on, I do not believe I would be able to maintain a dry eye."

My dry eyes looked directly into his. "Tears will not bring her back, Reverend."

"Mr. Constant… yet… uh…" I had thought him a man who never wanted for words. "Would you do me the pleasure of staying for our communal meal?" His eyebrows raised in query.

I needed to get back to the fields, as they would not plow themselves. "Perhaps another time, Reverend. I have chores to complete."

"But it is Sunday–the Lord's Day, the Sabbath. Men should not be toiling today!" His head tilted toward me. "Please join us." He gestured to the meeting house.

"Thank you mightily for your gracious invitation, but I must attend to my farm." I waved my hand as I walked away.

"We shall see each other next Sunday! Yes?" he called out.

The following Sunday I completed my chores just about the time the church service would have begun. After cleaning up, I felt a bit hungry and decided to attend the communal meal.

As I approached the table, Reverend Dickson stood and stepped toward me. "Mr. Constant! A delight! Please sit near me." He indicated an empty space on the bench from where he had risen.

"Reverend, if we are to associate, please call me by my Christian name, Azariah." I sat next to him. "Each time you say, 'Mr. Constant,' I am reminded of my deceased father."

"Yes, yes, of course. My apologies." He lifted a large platter. "Here, have some meat and bread."

Everyone else already had their portions and I did not feel squeamish about taking most of the remains. The meat could have been warmer, and the bread could have been softer, but I did not prepare the meal myself and had no standing to find fault.

Reverend Dickson took a swig from his mug and turned to me. "I saved a space for you, Azariah, because I had a feeling you might appear today." A smile on his pale lips gave flavor to my food.

"Thank you, sir. I had no inclination to attend until I realized the time and the rumbling in my belly." I smiled back at him and believed I saw a teardrop at the crease of his eye.

"And as you have requested me to call you Azariah, I equally insist you call me John." His hand rested upon my shoulder.

A dry piece of bread in my throat caught, and I coughed it back. "But Reverend, you and I are not on equal levels. You are my superior in both age and rank, sir."

"Perhaps, perhaps." He removed the hand from my shoulder and intertwined his fingers. "However, it is my prerogative to select how others shall call me, and I wish you to use *my* Christian name, John."

I nodded. "Indeed, it is an honor, John." Our gazes intertwined, and it felt as though I could see into the man's searching soul.

"You and I have something in common, Azariah," he muttered after pulling his eyes from mine. "I should say we probably have more in common than you might imagine."

He had me fascinated. "And what might that be, John?"

"Your father died in battle, as did my son, Peter. If I recall correctly, your father served with the British Army and fell near here. My Peter joined the Continental Forces and succumbed at Yorktown, just as the Revolution ended." Another tear formed.

Perhaps this distant connection propelled him to initiate some sort of association with me. His son died but two years past, and he had fought with the rebel forces. However, I suspected the reverend might have had other reasons to maintain a social bond. "I did not know of your boy, and I am aggrieved to hear of such. Mrs. Dickson must be mourning as well."

He turned away from me, ran a hand over his face, and then turned back. "Mrs. Dickson is no longer with us either. Peter had blond hair and blue eyes, just as you have." He stood. "Please excuse me."

I followed the black frock as it disappeared through a door.

Despite the amount of field work I performed the following week, I spent quite a bit of time considering the conversation I had with Reverend Dickson. I lacked a father, and he lacked a son. However, I could not help but consider there might have been some other, unspoken reason for his swift attachment to me.

My life had consisted of helping my parents with the farm. When my father died, I had to take over the duties of planting and reaping. With the recent passage of my mother, the housekeeping fell to me as well. Thoughts of finding someone to share a home with diminished as my workload increased.

Now and again, I caught myself taking in the likes of other fellows about my own age. None of the women in our town had drawn my eye. At first, I believed our local ladies did not possess the qualities I desired in a partner for life, but I eventually had to admit to myself that I preferred gentlemen to ladies.

The Reverend Dickson, although twenty years my senior, still appeared healthy and sound. Perhaps I might not have thought him attractive at first, following our conversation regarding our losses, my interest stirred. The men I had found myself gazing toward were also fair and blond, like me. John is darker in complexion and tresses. His flowing frock hides much of his physique, but I could sense the sinew and strength he commanded.

As Sunday approached, I searched my own soul for a reason not to return to the church. When I discovered none, I searched for a reason to go.

That came all too easily.

I planned my arrival to coincide with the end of the communal meal. Reverend Dickson stood collecting plates and cups.

"Ah, Azariah!" He set the pile atop a small table and walked toward me with an extended hand.

"John," I responded and took the offer of friendship. This time I did not shy away from him, and I intentionally held the handshake longer than the custom. My eyes studied his careworn face, and his glance dropped to the floor.

He cleared his throat and whispered, "Perhaps we should remove ourselves to the rectory, where we can speak with more candor."

I nodded and assisted with the collection of tableware. Once we had placed all the used objects in a washtub, the reverend led me to his humble home next door.

While the room included the bare essentials–a table, two chairs, a bed–it did not convey the sense of a proper house. Lacking a fireplace or stove, a chill fell upon me, and I pulled my coat tighter around me.

"It's not much, but it's home." His meager smile warmed me. "When Peter departed to join the army, I left my previous place nearby and began living here." Even though Spring had proceeded well, the weather had not yet reached a pleasant degree. I began to shiver. "Are you not warm enough, Azariah?"

Perhaps his long, black robe provided the protection from the cold he required. He went to the various windows, pulled the draperies closed and stepped to me. The reverend put his arms about my shoulders. The chill faded away.

"Thank you, John. I appreciate you taking an interest in my welfare."

He leaned back with a grin and a keen look in his eye. "Thank you for sparking my interest."

I had not kissed anyone but relations. In imaginations I had wanted to kiss plenty of others. For the first time in my life, I placed my chapped lips to those of another man, with my eyes closed. We stood holding on to each other for what seemed the longest time.

"Are you not happy with my appearance, Azariah?" he inquired when we detached.

"What are you asking, John?"

His finger aimed at my face. "You had closed your eyes and I had wondered if my old visage displeased you." He pointed to his own.

"No! Oh, no!" My hand went to my mouth. "Heavens, no!" I turned aside. "It's just that I had no idea what to do."

Without looking at him directly, I could sense his smile. "Is this the first time you have kissed another man?" I nodded. "Was there pleasure in it?" I hesitated, then nodded again. "Good! Let us continue."

Confusion addled my baffled brain. I had no expectations of how this interview would conduct itself. Fear and dread tightened my chest and I ran from the rectory, leaving the door open behind me. I could hear the reverend calling out my name through the wind in my ears.

Many of my thoughts the following week went to the brief episode in Reverend Dickson's home. I had finally kissed another man, albeit not be one of the ones I would have preferred. At length, I realized we both had unmet needs: he had lost a son, and I, a father. In my own soul, I recognized the preference for company of men to women, but I could not be sure of the reverend. He had been married and produced an heir.

When Sunday arrived, I had made up my mind to pursue the matter further. Instead of sitting through a service and the communal meal, I waited until the congregation had left and the reverend returned to his rectory.

Before knocking upon his door, I took two deep breaths to steel my nerve. My actions might cause anger, or they might result in joy. I believed myself prepared for either outcome. He answered with a stern expression, and my heart crumpled. Perhaps this decision had not been well thought through.

"Azariah!" The ends of his lips curled up and his eyes glimmered. "I do not get many visitors, and your presence is a very pleasant surprise, indeed." He opened the door fully and waved a hand. "Do, please, come in."

"Thank you, Reverend… John," I responded as I entered.

He directed us to sit at the table. "I was not quite sure whether I would ever see you again after our last encounter." A smile absorbed his face. "This social call, while unexpected, brings much relief to me, as I felt I might have transgressed our friendship and caused great harm to your spirit."

"But it was I who initiated the transgression, John. It was I who planted my lips upon yours."

"Yes. However, I fostered your action and carry equal blame, if any blame need be assigned." He took my hand, and I did not pull mine away. "Perhaps we are both culpable."

My gaze fell to the tabletop. "But you were married and fathered a son. Has your nature transmuted so as to be engaged with a man?"

His finger lifted my chin so that our eyes met. "My nature has never changed. I have always valued the closeness of other males. Our society expects men like me to take a wife, and I fulfilled that expectation to the best of my ability. The situation has shifted, and that obligation no longer stands."

We pulled each other's arms across the table, bringing our lips together once again. At first, my eyes closed on instinct, and when I realized this, parted my lids. His eyes smiled back at me. I had never known such delight.

When I had caught my breath, I asked, "I am not a person of faith, but is this not against your religious beliefs?"

He laughed as a child might, leaned forward, and kissed my cheek with delicacy. "No. It is not."

"But the Bible says –"

"The Bible says many things to many people. What the Good Book tells me is all that matters. In every bit of my teachings, I have never read a passage that prohibits love."

"Love?" I balked. "Do not your commandments forbid such love?"

His head bent down. "The commandments contain no such proscription. In fact, the words attributed to our Lord Jesus mention nothing of it."

I grabbed his wrist, "But what about Leviticus? Surely, there is a mention there."

"Yes." He nodded. "Leviticus contains many instructions to the wandering tribes. The Hebrew Bible orders us to circumcise our babies, but we no longer do that. It disallows eating shellfish or the flesh of animals that do not chew their cud and have cloven hooves, yet we enjoy ham from swine and clams from the shore."

He caught my glance. "Those laws were meant for a small band of religious refugees, not for civilized folks such as ourselves."

"And St. Paul's epistles?" I dropped his wrist.

"You certainly know your Bible well for someone who does not profess to cleave to religion." A stern face responded to my question. "However, Paul wrote his communiqués in a language no longer spoken. Subsequent translators have twisted his words to suit their particular sentiments." The frown transformed to a smile. "I, however, choose my own interpretation, and none of it speaks to the situation at hand." He grasped mine.

As my beliefs regarding our nascent love continued to fall together, this man of the cloth appeared resolute and at peace with his innermost feelings. I observed his venerating face and smiled from my depths. He applied his lips to mine, and I remembered to hold my eyes open. We gazed through each other's soul portals, and I felt my heart beating as never before.

Our session of sexual congress lasted until the candle had nearly extinguished. As I had no prior experience in such matters, I trusted John to lead as I followed. We pleasured each other and lay exhausted in his small bed.

He looked down upon me and spoke. "It is good, Azariah."

"It *is* good, John," I concurred.

"I'm not sure if you know the significance of your name." He rolled to my side, and I moved to face him.

"It is from the Bible, is it not?"

He nodded. "The prophet Azariah went to King Asa and encouraged him to carry out a set of reforms, including the destruction of idols in the Temple at Jerusalem and restoration of the sacrificial altar." A grin appeared. "The name means: 'He who helps God.'"

"And am I helping you as well?" I smirked.

"More than you could ever imagine."

For many years I visited Reverend John Dickson on Sunday. Sometimes I sat through his service. Other times I attended only for the communal meal. Habitually, we repaired to the rectory for an afternoon of shared affections. After a while I began thinking to myself of these encounters, with a bit of humor, as "Sinday."

Following our congress sessions, John would look into my eyes and state, "It is good, Azariah." That made me feel better about myself than anything else in the whole sum of my inconsequential world.

We never knew if the townspeople learned the true nature of our relationship. Such chatter did not concern us. Beyond the initial meeting of a sonless father and a fatherless son from opposite sides of a common conflict, we developed a lasting and fast bond. Despite the difference in our ages—or, perhaps, because of it—no one ever mentioned my frequent Sunday/Sinday visits.

He lived two decades more before succumbing to the fever. My heart died as well, but the farm provided essential motivation to carry on.

190

At his funeral service, I sat in the same splintery pew and re-viewed my own thoughts while the new reverend droned on about my love's life and deeds. From the cold, stone building, I walked to the site of his fresh grave, looked down and said, "It is good, John. Truly, it is."

Out of Yoshiwara

This story, like *Noah's Raft*, had been written as a submission to *Best Gay Erotica of the Year*. We had seen a museum exhibition about Yoshiwara, the pleasure island off Edo, Japan, in the 18th Century. I found it fascinating and wanted to tell the story of male geishas. The editor declined because I had the characters speaking in a foreign language. With a bit of re-writing (and extended erotic scenes), the story made it into a later edition, along with one from my partner, Rick May, making us the first couple to have our works included in the same volume. This is the original version.

Out of Yoshiwara

In the Floating World
Where all things change
Love does change
When promising it never will change.

–Folk poem

Usagi Uchikina looked left, right, behind him, right, left and behind again before stepping tentatively from the Nihon-Zutsumi embankment onto the bridge crossing over to Yoshiwara. As the eldest son of a great shipping magnate, he had to be careful not to be observed going to the Floating World for his pleasure. This was the first time he actually set toe upon the slender causeway connecting Edo to the island of forbidden delights. His previous attempts stopped short of crossing because his niggling fears overcame his compelling desires.

Who might see me? Would anyone recognize me? Will I shame my father and his company if someone knows I have gone to Yoshiwara? His thoughts agonized between maintaining the good face of his family and satisfying his ever-increasing urges to be intimate with another man.

Had Uchikina been born with the interest in women that most other men had, he would not have had to resort to such stealthy

behaviors. He had heard there were other men who felt as he did–
and that he would probably find them in Yoshiwara–but as the
eldest son, and obvious heir, to a powerful merchant of the
Kitamaebune Northern Sea trade, he did not feel secure enough to
make public his particular preference for male companionship.

His family had built up their transport business over the last
three generations. If anything should happen to his father,
Uchikina would have to take over the running of the business.
While he considered himself prepared to seize those reins, should
the necessity arise, his thirtieth year would soon arrive, and an un-
married man of his age might appear improper or weak.

On the right side of the path he noticed a wishing well.
Uchikina quickly tossed a few *mon* coins for good fortune and hurried to the entry gate. He kept his head down in hopes that no one
would recognize him. The smoldering in his tender parts persisted
in motivating him forward.

At the gate, an old woman stopped him with her tiger gaze.
Her back bent, the tattered silk embroidered jacket nearly touching
the ground. "*NAN DESHŌ?*" she spat.

*What **do** I want? The question is expected, but the questioner is
unexpected. How can I explain?* Uchikina hesitated.

Dark brown spittle followed and dribbled down her wrinkled
chin. Again, she prompted, "*NAN DESHŌ?*"

The timid man looked left, right and behind him again. He
then peered into the face of the guardian of pleasures as she wiped
her chin with a sleeve.

Her eyes opened wide, becoming almost round in shape. Her cataracts clearly reflecting the light of the lantern overhead. "*USAGI-SAN?*" the woman asked warily.

How does she recognize me? Uchikina pondered. *I am wearing peasant clothes and the pilgrim hat worn by samurai to conceal their forbidden visits to the Floating City.*

Uchikina nodded carefully, barely moving his head.

A wise smile crossed the old woman's face. "*ANATA WA GEISHA DESU?*" she goaded.

No, I do not wish to have a **woman** *for pleasure*, he thought. *I desire another man for my time here.*

He shook his head slightly. "*OTOKO,*" he whispered.

"*ANO… OTOKO GEISHA DESU,*" she nodded, touching a bony finger to her nose. The old woman turned and began walking into the walled city. After a few steps, she motioned for Uchikina to follow.

'No tipping, please.' Uchikina read the sign posted on the pillar at the first intersection. *How strange. If one is to receive excellent service, tipping should be essential.*

They walked past two main lanes. Along the way, the man saw paintings on the walls of people engaged in sexual activities, many of them forbidden back in Edo. At some of the paintings, men sat with their robes open, pleasuring themselves while studying the enticing artwork. Seeing other men touching themselves aroused Uchikina, and a small bulge formed at the front of his gown.

"*MATTE!*" barked the old woman, "*ANATA GA MATTE!*" and she slapped at his crotch.

She wants me to wait. For what? Have I made the wrong decision? Uchikina considered. He stopped and contemplated running back to the safety of Edo. But before he could move, the scrawny old woman grabbed his wrist with unexpected strength and pulled him toward a door a few paces off the main walkway.

After knocking gently, the woman slid a small panel at her eye level open and whispered a few words. She stepped back and pointed to the opening.

Uchikina stood, unable to move, paralyzed with fear.

Again, the bony woman grabbed him by the wrist and pulled him up to the door and pointed through the small opening. When Uchikina dared to look, he saw a set of beautiful eyes looking back at him.

These are pretty eyes. Decorated with alluring paints.

"*OTOKO DESU KA?*" He turned to his companion.

She nodded curtly and responded, "*HAI, DANSEI GEISHA DESU.*" Her smile revealed the browning teeth beneath her leathery lips, and she nodded again.

He is a man, but his eyes appear quite feminine. I wonder if this is the one she has picked out for me. Uchikina pointed to himself and his eyebrows raised in question.

The woman spat and commanded, "*ANATA WA ASHITA MADE MATANAKEREBA NARIMASEN!*"

198

Tomorrow? Why must I wait until tomorrow? I have risked the reputation of my esteemed family to cross the bridge to Yoshiwara for this one night. Would I be able to risk another?

Before he had a chance to verbalize any question or objection, the old woman slammed the panel closed, grabbed Uchikina's wrist and pulled him back to the entrance. "*Ashita!*" she directed, letting go of the wrist and pushing him toward the bridge.

As he walked back to the family home nearby, he contemplated his strategy for the following evening and how to return to this place without anyone else discovering his secret longings.

The next night, feigning illness, Uchikina excused himself from the family dinner and went to his rooms. He changed into the peasant costume, and, after a few minutes, moved stealthily to the door and let himself out into a star-filled night.

After crossing the bridge yet again, he encountered the same grandmother from the previous visit. Upon seeing him, the old woman whispered, "*Usagi-san. Sore wa anata ni mōichido aeru koto o ureshiku omoimasu.*" She bowed slightly.

I wish she would not show deference to me in front of others. He glanced about, but no one seemed to be looking at them. *Perhaps others of high rank also disguised themselves as well, and my appearance is not out of the ordinary at all.* He smiled down at her. *And she says she is happy to see me again. That is also welcome information.*

"*Anata wa okurimono o motte kimashita ka?*" she looked up and inquired.

A gift? How was I supposed to know I had to bring a gift? How complicated the rules of Yoshiwara and the ways of the Geisha. "DON'NA OKURIMONO O MOTTE KONAKEREBA NARANAI NODESU KA?" Ushikina asked. If he was supposed to bring something, he should at least know what to purchase.

Dim slights played off her glazed eyes. "HANA O MOTTE KITE KUDASAI."

Flowers? Yes. I guess that sounds reasonable. "HANA DESU," Uchikina acknowledged.

The woman grabbed his wrist again but gently, as if to confide, not to constrain. "ANATA WA HANAKOTOBA O RIKAI SHITE IMASU KA?"

'HANAKOTOBA?' The language of flowers. Of course, everything must have a meaning, and I must select the appropriate blossom to convey my intentions. Uchikina nodded his comprehension. "HANA WA WATASHI NO ITO O TSUTAERU HITSUYŌ GA ARIMASU."

She bowed again and pointed back across the bridge.

At the market along the lantern-lined Nihon-Zutsumi embankment, Uchikina sought the flower merchant. The meanings of most of the flowers were known: TSUBAKI, the Camelia, meant 'humility,' but he wanted to display more desire; SUMIRE, the Violet, in the shape of an ink jar, communicated 'small love or bliss,' but he wanted to be bolder; SAKURA, the Cherry Blossom, the very symbol of their country, said 'accomplishment,' but he had yet to accomplish anything; ASAGAO, the Morning Glory, means 'brief love,' not exactly the message he had intended; UME, the

Apricot Blossom, with its five-petal pink flower, meant 'elegance,' but the Yoshiwara did not seem the appropriate place. He considered the *KINMOKUSEI*, Osmanthus, for a brief time because it demonstrated 'nobility,' but then he realized he did not want to divulge his rank at first meeting.

Among all the lovely blooms presented, it was *MOMO*, the Peach Blossom, and its lovely pink, frilly petals, that conveyed his intention. *Fascination. Commitment. Romance. That sounds like the message I should want to convey.* He paid for the arrangement and walked back to Yoshiwara, diligent as always for fear that his disguise should be penetrated and he be discovered, thus dishonoring his family.

The old woman, gatekeeper of Yoshiwara, smiled upon seeing the gift Uchikina had procured. Instead of grabbing his wrist, she bowed and led him along the main path through the intersecting little streets.

Like the previous evening, men sat along the walkway admiring the artwork and pleasuring themselves. Uchikina attempted not to look at this activity lest he become aroused again, and he did not wish for the old woman to touch his personal area yet another time.

They arrived at the same door of the same room as the night before. After knocking and sliding open the panel, the same set of eyes looked out again, this time they appeared to be smiling. The woman took the flowers from Uchikina and held up them up for inspection.

"HAI. SORE WA TOTEMO YOI DESU," came a whispered response through the view hole.

The gift is acceptable! I am pleased! Perhaps we can move to the next step now.

The old woman slid the panel closed again, and Uchikina scowled at her.

Now what? When do I get to meet this alluring person?

"ASHITA. ANATA WA ASHITA MODOTTE KITE, OCHA O NOMIMASU," the woman whispered.

Tomorrow? For tea? Uchikina had difficulty accepting the long, slow process for meeting his intended Geisha. He summoned up all the resolve he could muster and exhaled slowly. *"ASHITA. ASHITA DENAKEREBA NARANAI,"* he whined.

"ANATA WA OCHA O HARAU HITSUYŌ GA ARIMASU!"

Of course, I will have to pay for the tea. I have already paid for the flowers. I have invested so much of my time and money already, and I will need to plan another deception for tomorrow.

The old woman pointed back toward the entrance. She did not accompany Uchikina this time. He walked with his face to the ground the entire way home.

During the next day, Uchikina's father approached and inquired as to his son's health. Uchikina had almost forgotten about his ruse from the prior evening, feigning illness. When he expressed feeling better, his father looked at him sideways, instructed him to bring another flower this evening, winked, and then walked away.

My father knows where I am going! Uchikina realized, *but he does not know why. Perhaps all men my age are drawn to Yoshiwara, and my father recognized my behavior as being similar to that of his own when he was younger.*

That evening, on the way to the bridge, Uchikina stopped at the flower merchant and purchased a corsage of Camelias, which expressed humility. The sweet scent of the petals reminded him of his innocent childhood, playing in the garden. As the son of an important man, he had no responsibilities until he began school, and the memory of his youth smelled of Camelias.

This night, with the moon peeking over his shoulder, Uchikina had chosen to return again to Yoshiwara in hopes of meeting a mate, a partner, another soul to share a life with.

The old woman smiled at the gift and led him to a different room this time. She slid open a rice-paper wall panel and indicated to go inside.

Uchikina peered in and saw two pillows with a small table be-tween them. *I shall be having tea with my Geisha tonight!*

He carried the corsage into the room and sat on one of the pillows. The woman smiled, bowed and retreated, closing the panel behind her. Around the room on various tables sat bonsai arrangements, cinnabar statues, incense burners and ivory lamps. Hanging on the wall he could see scrolls of poetry written in fancy characters.

A few minutes later, the panel slid open again, and a young fellow wearing the dull clothing of a businessman entered. Uchikina recognized him but said nothing, fearing he would give away his identity. He merely bowed from the waist in mock deference to his rank inferior.

Once the young man sat, the panel slid closed again. The two looked in opposite directions, attempting to avoid any chance of looking at each other.

Without warning, another panel opened. However, this panel was solid bamboo, made to look like part of the wall. *A secret doorway!*

Through the entrance stepped a beautifully-dressed figure: purple silk kimono, the distinctive flat red cap of pleasure bringers atop layers of loosely-braided hair with dangling strings of cherry blossoms, delicate feet in white hose on tall, oval-shaped bamboo *okobos*. The ceremonial bow was performed so deeply, it looked like the geisha might drop the tea tray and topple from the elevated shoes. Jasmine-scented steam filled the air.

The Geisha placed a small porcelain cup on the table for both men and then filled each halfway. The young businessman peered into the half-filled cup and then glared at the Geisha, as if to say, 'Where is the rest of my tea?'

The Geisha picked up the Camelia corsage, smiled ever so slightly, and attached it to one wrist. Uchikina looked up at the Geisha with a blank expression. *That was supposed to have been for my special person! But I cannot ask for it back. That would not be proper. Now, what shall I do?*

The Geisha bowed again and backed out of the room, closing the bamboo panel afterward. The two men sat in silence, not looking at each other. Uchikina reached for the cup in front of him, but it proved too hot to pick up, and he left it on the table. The other fellow grabbed his own tea and poured it down his throat with no ceremony.

It is no wonder he is a junior businessman. He has no manners.

A few minutes later, the old woman slid open the rice-paper panel. The younger man stood quickly, placed a few coins in her hand and rushed out with an angry scowl. Uchikina went to take some coins from his pocket, but the woman shook her head side-to-side and held up a flat palm.

"*ASHITA?*" he asked.

She nodded in the affirmative. *Tomorrow...*

Uchikina felt the cup again, and it had cooled sufficiently for drinking, and he sipped the Jasmine tea with gratitude. When he had finished, the woman bid him good night and escorted him back to the entrance.

As he walked home, chasing his shadow, he worried that the other fellow might have recognized him and tell the rest of the world about his socially-unacceptable desires.

Uchikina remembered the Cherry Blossoms in the Geisha's hair, and he stopped at the flower merchant to purchase a few strands of braided flowers. He hoped their message of 'accomplishment' proved strong enough to move the meeting process forward.

At the gate, the old woman smiled at the gift and then wiped some brown spittle from her wrinkled mouth. She nodded her head to the main walkway, and Uchikina followed. They stopped outside the same room as the previous evening. He looked down at the old woman for some sign as to what would happen this time as the rice-paper panel slid open. She nodded, pushed him inside and slid the door closed.

Alone, Uchikina had only his fear-drenched thoughts for company. *I have waited many nights for this moment, but now I am not sure what I want anymore. This is not right. I am a bad person. Why can't I be like the others? I cannot stay here.*

He moved toward the door just as the secret panel opened on the other side of the room. In stepped the same beautifully-dressed figure with the purple silk kimono, flat red cap, and bamboo okobos. The Geisha slid the bamboo panel closed.

That old woman must have misunderstood. I do not want a female Geisha. This was a bad idea. I must leave. Now! He stepped toward the door, but the intruder jumped in front of him, took the braid of Cherry Blossoms, and pointed strongly to the tatami mat on the floor.

Uchikina stared at the authoritative figure and shriveled inside. Weak and impotent, his head hung like a drooping plum, wilting under its own weight. He couldn't even walk out of a tearoom under his own volition. *Failure!* he thought of himself. *The*

Cherry Blossoms are a lie! With no further resistance, he sat on the floor as directed as the Geisha fastened the flowers to the wig.

A fan appeared from the robe's sleeve, and the stranger began dancing, undulating in precise motions: a hip thrust, an arm lunge, opening and closing the fan, a head tilt. The tassel hanging from the fan swung around like a fish on a line and Uchikina followed its hypnotizing motions not knowing what to do in this uncomfortable situation. *I will have spent my father's money for nothing!*

The fan disappeared back into the sleeve and the figure advanced, pushing him down onto the mat in a sitting position. Uchikina reluctantly allowed himself to be ordered around. When the bare skin of a hand touched his neck, an unpredictable swelling began again. As he landed on the mat, the hand caressed his ear, and the swelling continued.

Why am I aroused? This does not make sense! His thoughts raced.

Two hands now rubbed his shaven crown, stimulating the bare skin. Sex juice began to form at the tip of his *bokki*. He actually enjoyed this! When the Geisha gently pulled on the topknot, audible sighs escaped from the quivering lips of the terrified man.

With his eyes closed, Uchikina imagined a man touching him in this manner. While it was not specifically sexual, it was very exciting. Just as he began to picture the face of his young, male page-boy, something hit him in the nose.

He opened his eyes to see a bulge in the front of the geisha's kimono. Instinctively he reached up to touch the interruption, but his hand got slapped away. *Is the womanly figure before me actually a man?* Uchikina looked up into the face of the other and asked, "*WAKASHŪ?*"

The geisha nodded in the affirmative. That explained why Uchikina found this intimacy arousing: His geisha was a young man! More juices flowed and an imperceptible stain began to form inside his fundoshi.

In a rare act of self-disclosure, he pointed to himself and said, "*UCHIKINA.*"

"*KAWAI,*" came the whispered response. The boy then pointed to the mat again.

Uchikina laid down, more comfortable with his partner. Kawai began to remove the customer's peasant clothes used as a disguise. Now, wearing only the fundoshi, Uchikina rested flat on the tatami and relaxed like a baby in his mother's arms.

The attendant moved a water basin to the side of the mat and began the ritual cleansing. Uchikina tried to relax as much as possible, but when the young fellow began undoing the last piece of clothing, his undergarment, it proved too much for him. *I am not ready for this!* No man had ever touched him in an intimate way before. Uchikina reached to dissuade the other from continuing.

From inside a hidden pocket, Kawai produced a red cord and began gently tethering Uchikina's hands and wrists together, palms facing, as if in greeting. The erection pulsed harder with each brush of skin.

He could feel the sullied fundoshi being untied, but the cloth still lay beneath him on the tatami. The young man resumed the bathing, this time swabbing Uchikina's private area. The cold water felt uncomfortable. "*IH, IH*" muttered the anxious man being bathed. When Kawai pulled back the loose skin of his penis and dabbed the cloth on the sensitive head, it felt like the push of a great river against a dam, wanting to burst forth and flow. Each swipe of the wet cloth brought him one step closer to finality.

Eventually the bath ended and Uchikina could relax a bit, knowing he was clean and ready for the erogenous pleasures to come. Kawai then removed a stalk of cherry blossoms from his hair and began stroking Uchikina's chest up and down, back and forth. When Kawai leaned over and licked a nipple, cries of delight sprang from Uchikina's mouth. The young man smiled a little.

Next, Kawai sat across Uchikina's waist and slipped his delicate legs under and around the calves of the paying customer. The gentle pressure of the intertwining limbs and the smooth stockings across his bare flesh added to the excitement and more juice dribbled.

Kawai stood, and seeing the dab of goo shining at the tip of Uchikina's penis, he touched the fluid with his finger and then swabbed it across his dainty, outstretched tongue. A grin of appreciation curved his mouth, and Uchikina smiled back awkwardly in discomfiture. Kawai continued to savor the taste of his client's juice.

The youth then gently folded one of Uchikina's legs so that it bent at the hip and knee.

SLAP!!!

"*Ai!*" cried Uchikina.

SLAP!!!

The boy kept smacking the man's bony rump with an open palm.

SLAP!!!

This is supposed to be pleasurable, thought Uchikina, but then he realized his penis strained and the juices flowed even more than before. *Why am I enjoying this so much? What is wrong with me?*

A ticklish feeling began to overshadow the sting of the slaps. Kawai had picked up the feather of a peafowl, long and wispy, and he now swiped the delicate threads over Uchikina's reddened buttock. The feather brushing continued up his chest, across his neck, down his side, between his thighs, and along the length of his taut manhood. An unbearable pressure had built up inside him and he was about to discharge.

The tap on his erection, and the shaking of Kawai's head, prevented the premature release of his pent-up sex. Kawai smiled with only half of his mouth, and Uchikina closed his eyes, ultimately giving up any control over the situation. With his hands tied, Uchikina could not touch his partner as his urges dictated. *I must do my part to satisfy. Please! Let me caress you.*

Uchikina flinched the first time Kawai touched his testicles directly. "*AH, AH!*" he muttered, but the young fellow continued giving pleasure to his assigned man. The graceful fingers traced the curves of the sac, the little wrinkles, playfully lifting and dropping each golden egg in turn. Uchikina's desire increased with each touch, and every time he felt the release approach, Kawai tapped the penis, training its master not to succumb too quickly.

After four or five close calls, the finger wandered down to Uchikina's hole, a place no one had ever touched before, not even his family physician. "*OH, OH*," he cried as the boy's dainty finger circled the chrysanthemum opening. He could feel the wet juice from his erection drip onto his lower abdomen. *How much longer can he tempt me? I must finish!*

Again, four or five taps kept Uchikina from early completion, and the finger began to poke through the band of muscle, wiggling as it penetrated. "*UH, UH!*" whispered the satisfied customer. After a few minutes, Kawai had an entire exploratory finger inside the warm cavity, and more taps had to be administered.

Without warning, the finger withdrew abruptly. Uchikina opened his eyes to see Kawai stepping to the door and leaving. *I hope this is no trick to catch me in disgrace and bring shame upon my family.* Even the doubting thoughts could not cause a reduction in the purple swelling.

A few moments later, the boy returned with a dish of shaved ice and a silver spoon. He closed the door again and knelt next to Uchikina, offering a spoonful of frozen water. It refreshed the sweat-covered man instantly. He held his mouth open, begging for another scoop. Kawai dipped the spoon into the porcelain bowl and brought a mound of ice near to Uchikina's mouth but would not let him eat it. The man strained his neck to reach the spoon, but the insolent boy kept moving it away, bit by bit. After an eternity of taunting, the cold ice fell into the waiting mouth, like a mother bird feeding its nestlings.

Uchikina licked his lips and smiled at the satisfaction. Suddenly he felt something very cold at the other end. "*EH, EH?*" blurted the man as Kawai placed a scoop of ice on Uchikina's penis. The sensation felt unusual, but as it was all part of the treatment, Uchikina just allowed the practiced young fellow to continue his repertoire.

Next, the warm, moist mouth covered Uchikina's erection. It was almost too great a pleasure as a tongue teased the sensitive parts, plucking the cord, lapping lightly at the sagging testicles and drumming the swollen head. Again, as the threshold approached, Kawai withdrew, but instead of taps or slaps, icy water from the bowl of ice drizzled down his penis and onto his ball sac.

"*AI!*" Uchikina howled. Kawai half-smiled again and continued alternating warm and moist with cold and wet.

This is most pleasurable! I cannot believe I have waited so long to treat myself to such things. What an idiot I have been, mused the man dripping in his own juices.

Once again Kawai used his mouth on Uchikina, but after a minute he took the last bits of ice left in the bowl and inserted them quickly into the butthole of his writhing customer.

The man spasmed and jerked. So much stimulation! The warm and moist in front contrasted with the freezing cold in the back. *So much torture! So much pleasure!*

When Uchikina felt Kawai step away, he opened his eyes again. The boy began to disrobe slowly and deliberately. He desperately wanted to stroke himself as he watched the beautiful young man reveal himself in ritualistic choreography. Unfortunately, his hands were tied so that he could not reach the desired spot. However, his erection continued to pulse with delight at the visual stimulation.

First the obi, which he folded ceremoniously before placing it on a low table. Next, the silk kimono, with its intricate, flowery design of silver threads piercing the purple cloth, slid like a glacier from the shoulders and arms, revealing ivory skin beneath. Two brown alluring circlets decorated his flat chest. Kawai slipped off the red crepe woman's undergarment he wore instead of a fundoshi, and his large member poked out precipitously, like a curved halberd. Lastly, he stepped off the okobos, losing a few inches of height. *What a vision!*

Once he returned, he massaged Uchikina's penis with his tongue a few times to rekindle the passion. As the man once again neared climax, Kawai stopped the stimulation and spat profusely into his hands. Using the saliva as lubricant, he swabbed his own magnificent piece and placed the tip at Uchikina's tender hole.

No! No! thought Uchikina, unable to speak. *I am the man. I must not be penetrated!*

With his curious half-smile, Kawai raised Uchikina's heels and plunged resolutely into the waiting abyss.

Waves of pain cut into Uchikina, like a katana Samurai attack. It hurt; it felt unbelievably good. He wanted it out; he wanted it never to leave.

Then the thrusting began. Over and over and over and over, the boy with the large man root drove his piston in and out. Sweat began to pour down Kawai's painted forehead as he cultivated his own enjoyment. His long braids swayed as if a breeze blew through the cubicle, and the strings of cherry blossoms swung like the tails of agitated cats.

Uchikina felt ashamed by the onslaught, and tears formed in his eyes. *I am eternally damned and no one will ever look upon me with favor again.*

The tempo of the pounding increased and slowed, increased and slowed for what seemed an hour. Both of them sweat like a bath house full of hogs, squealing and squawling.

Finally, Uchikina felt the moist tongue of Kawai upon his engorged member again. This time, nothing could hold him back, and rocket after rocket of his male soup shot into the boy's voracious mouth, potentially drowning and choking him.

Kawai gave one last plunge and Uchikina could feel a river pouring out of his backyard crack, sticky and slimy. The young fellow collapsed on top of him, heaving and sighing.

I wish I could hug him, but my hands are restrained, thought Uchikina. *This experience has been most delightful, and I shall have to find a way to tip the boy, even though the practice is forbidden.*

The young fellow slowly moved off of Uchikina and knelt by his side, as if in prayer or meditation. After a few seconds of stillness, Kawai moved to retrieve the peahen feather, and he began to stroke it up and down the man's thighs and waltzing it across his groin.

Oh, praise Buddha, there is more! Uchikina smiled. *I had no idea what services were to be provided.*

Once the stirring of the customer's shriveled rod began again, Kawai took it in his mouth and began to practice his oral calisthenics. Within a minute, Uchikina was hard and dripping once more. As his restraint was still in place, he merely relaxed, trusting the boy as he had never trusted anyone before.

Just as in the previous session, Kawai brought him to the brink a few times, tapping the customer's ready erection to prevent the end. After a few minutes of this blissful torture, the young man spit profusely into his hands.

Oh, no. Not again, Uchikina feared. My tender parts still ache.

He opened his mouth, about to object, but the young fellow put a saliva-laden finger to the man's lip to silence the protestation.

Uchikina realized, *I must trust that he will not hurt me.*

Again, the boy produced profuse saliva into his hands, but this time he applied it to his customer's penis.

"*MMMMM*," purred Uchikina.

Kawai positioned himself above the ready lance and slowly lowered himself down until his tailbones rested upon Uchikina's hips.

"*AHHHHHHH*," sighed Uchikina.

I have never penetrated another, he mused. *So delightful!*

The boy began to swivel about, grinding his bottom on the man's groin and pressing his palms against the man's chest.

"*OHHHHHHH*," moaned Uchikina.

And finally the raising and lowering began. Slowly at first, allowing the client to nearly approach climax but not permitting that pleasure too soon. Once the feeling subsided, the boy began the sweet torture again, varying speeds, up and down, up and down, up and down.

"*ARR, ARR, ARRRRRRR!*" groaned Uchikina, wishing the young fellow would just let him finish, but realizing that the prolonging of pleasure was all part of the performance.

He glanced down and saw Kawai's massive penis bobbing around. It had been soft before, but now it had fully hardened and pointed toward Uchikina's face.

Soft squeaks of delight escaped the boy's throat as he clawed at his client's chest and bounced off his hips faster and faster and faster. Suddenly, jets of juice slammed into Uchikina's nose, eyes and mouth. The rhythmic contractions of Kawai's anal muscles around his own penis propelled Uchikina over the brink, and he filled the young man's cavity with his own juices.

Because his own hands were tethered, he could do nothing to stop the burning sensation of his eyes and nose. However, the taste of his temporary partner's semen was a curious new sensation.

Hmm, slightly salty, slightly sweet. He lapped his lips to get every drop.

Kawai reached for a damp cloth and patted Uchikina's face to cleanse it. He then looked down into his customer's eyes and both smiled simultaneously and unexpectedly. The youth spoke, "*DOMO ARIGATO, SENSEI,*" in a deep male voice.

Uchikina's eyebrows raised at hearing the feminine-looking boy speak with a man's tone. "*DOMO, KAWAI,*" he groaned and grinned.

After a few more moments of exchanged smiles, the young man stood, dropped the cloth, grabbed his kimono and donned it. He motioned for Uchikina to stay put and he left the cubicle once more.

Perhaps I was wrong about this place after all. Who knew what pleasures were to be found here? If only I could have had the courage to come to Yoshiwara before. If only I could have someone like Kawai at home... If only... Uchikina's thoughts rushed through his head.

The young fellow returned with a basin of warm water and a few cloths. He began bathing Uchikina ceremoniously and he also removed the red cord from the man's wrists. Once he completed the bath of his customer, he turned the attention to himself.

Uchikina started to rise, dressing himself in the disguise he had worn to conceal his true identity. He gazed down upon the person who had just brought him the supreme pleasures he had sought in coming to Yoshiwara. Kawai paused his cleansing briefly to look upward with moist and fluttering eyes. The client began to realize that if he did nothing, this spectacular specimen might be taken on by another patron, never to be seen again.

Love, much like tipping, is frowned upon in Yoshiwara. However, this fortunate opportunity is too great to risk losing. Perhaps I can put him on our payroll and house him at the employee apartments. He could be my page-boy's assistant.

With a smile just a bit too emotional, Uchikina looked at Kawai, who smiled back bashfully but quickly averted his face.

How utterly lovely! He must wait here for me while I conduct the business. "*ANATA WA MATTE,*" he instructed Kawai as he slid the door opened and disappeared.

As the customer left the cubicle, the young man smiled, completely and thoroughly, for he believed he knew what was to transpire. In no particular hurry, he dressed himself in his geisha outfit, repainted his face and knelt on the floor, waiting for the next move.

On his way back to the front gate, Uchikina again noticed the personal sex acts of others studying the erotic art. This time, it did not divert his attention because he had a mission in mind and nothing would interfere.

He inquired of the old woman at the entrance how he could acquire Kawai, paying off his indebtedness, and bring him into his own household. The sly gatekeeper smiled at Uchikina and winked, indicating she knew she had done her job well and made a good match for her newest client.

The two merchants swiftly struck a deal, and Uchikina paid gladly. Now he could have a person in his life who appeared to the world as a woman, but in the privacy of their own rooms, well…

Uchikina walked back to the cubicle with a light step, almost giddy at his luck. He slid the door open and saw his sensual delight sitting, waiting patiently. He reached down, and Kawai reached up, placing a delicate hand in the masculine grasp, allowing his new master to assist with standing.

This situation is most pleasing. I can enjoy my sex with Kawai in private, but yet in public, people will see him as a woman companion. Uchikina smiled. *But something is not yet correct.* He visually scrutinized his new acquisition. *Of course!* He reached over and removed the red cap from Kawai's hair, an obvious indicator of his renounced profession. The boy smiled at the attention.

The man looked down and saw the gaudy okobo platforms on which Kawai balanced. *We shall have to obtain some proper shoes, but for now, I hope the kimono is long enough to hide them.* He tugged at and adjusted the soft silk robe so that it hung as low as possible, and the shoes of the geisha disappeared from view.

Hand-in-hand, the two walked proudly out the gate. Uchikina stopped and tossed a few more coins into the well, hoping to further increase his bounty of luck. He grasped Kawai's hand again, and the two of them walked onto the Nihon-Zutsumi embankment as any Japanese couple would.